I0523714

Two Hearts And A Villa

Billionaire Romance Series (Book 2)

Lucy Appadoo

Copyright© 2024 Lucy Appadoo

All rights reserved. No part of this publication may be reproduced, stored in a retrieval system, or transmitted in any form or by any means, electronic or mechanical, including photocopying, recording without either the prior permission in writing from the publisher as expressly permitted by law, or under the terms agreed.

The author's moral rights have been asserted.

This book is dedicated to those who trust in love. The complications are worth it.

Contents

CHAPTER 1

The scent of flowers warmed her heart as Rose Terrini stared at the wilting green stems of the crimson, red, and yellow roses inside the vase on the kitchen table. She leaned forward, her elbows resting on the table. Five other vases of flowers were placed around the living room, and a pile of small notes of condolences were piled high on the kitchen counter. Reminders of her great aunt, Maria, who had died two weeks earlier.

Rose sat between her friends, Dalia on her right, and Gina on her left.

"How are you feeling?" asked Dalia, threading her hands through her copper-coloured hair, which fell below her shoulders. Her chestnut eyes and narrow nose enhanced her beauty. She gazed at her friend and arched her brow.

Rose's back ached as she rested against the hard back of the chair, her chest heavy, a hot tear sliding down her cheek. Her hands trembled as she stared past her friend. "I loved Maria so much. She still had another ten years in her, I'm sure, Dals."

Her friend nodded.

Gina's brown eyes darkened, her posture rigid as she scrutinised Rose. "She's not suffering anymore."

Rose swallowed and glided a hand across her shaky leg, her heart palpitating. The silence in those moments stretched out as her friends bowed and remained quiet. She couldn't dwell on the loss as what good would it do? Instead, she focused on her upcoming trip and brushed aside her grief. As much as she wanted to cry her heart out in her room just then, she had to pick herself up and get on with things. She wasn't the type to wallow in sadness. Dear Maria would want her to move on.

She took a calming breath. "I've booked my trip to Montepulciano for next week."

Dalia squeezed her hand. "Are you sure you're ready to do that?" Rose nodded. "How do you feel about the proposal?"

Rose glanced at her hand, still visibly shaking. "I don't know. It's something I don't want to be dealing with after...Maria..." She scratched the back of her neck. "Without seeing the villa, it's hard to decide whether I should sell it or not. My mum said that it's my choice since my dad transferred ownership of it to me." A vision of Maria's tight hug made her smile. "She knew how much I hated leaving Tuscany, but my parents knew there were more opportunities here."

Gina pursed her lips and pointed a bright red fingernail in the air. "It might be in pristine condition; you might decide not to sell." Her glossy, curled auburn hair flowed down to her shoulders, making her look like a top model.

Rose shrugged, thinking the same thing. "I'll find out for sure next week." She was glad to avoid the winter weather in Melbourne and replace it with summer in Tuscany for the month of June. "I imagine Maria would most likely have struggled to maintain it. She was eighty." Her hands rested across her chest as her breath deepened. "I remember living in that huge place: the four bedrooms, spacious balcony, and the breathtaking views."

Dalia smiled. "I cannot believe you and your parents lived there for eighteen years of your life. Would you really go back there to live?"

Rose swallowed. "As much as I loved Tuscany, Melbourne's my home now and I can't imagine leaving you guys or my mum." Gesturing towards her chest, her heart, she added, "But it is a chance to capture memories by writing about Tuscany in my travel blog."

"Isn't Italy more corrupt than here?" said Gina. "How safe is it?"

Rose sighed, knowing that Gina was the negative yet realistic one while Dalia had the creative and nurturing soul. "Isn't everywhere corrupt?"

"Oh, it's such a romantic place," said Dalia. "You should just go have a fling. Plenty of hot, single guys in Italy."

Rose's chest burned. "Oh, dream on, girl. There is no way I'm doing that. I have bigger things to focus on. Besides, all men are cut from the same cloth. I'm over it." Her ex-boyfriend, Hugh, came to mind. He had burned her so badly that she would no longer trust any man who made her feel worthless and insecure. The bastard had his secrets too. No way in hell.

"I agree with Dalia," said Gina. She peered past her. "Why not enjoy yourself, Rose? You have been under a lot of pressure lately. You can let yourself go..."

Rose scoffed. "Right. I don't see you doing that, Gina." Lifting her shoulders, she said, "No flings, and that's that."

Dalia wrinkled a brow. "What about your Mum? Wouldn't she want to go to Italy with you?"

Rose exhaled, thinking how hard it was for her mother to accept her leaving. Italy reminded her of her late father. "She's fine with it now, but it took at least a week for her not to be reminded of my dad and how they fell in love over there. She has her job and said she's too busy, but in truth, she can't cope with the memories. Even now, she still refuses to move on and find someone new. She's still young; in her fifties. It's been eight years since he died."

"I hear you," said Dalia. "But there is no timeline for grief. Your mother might be young, but she obviously hasn't met the right man."

Rose didn't want to think about the similar traits she shared with her mother: independent, ambitious, outgoing, perfectly fine without a man. She got up. "I have to start packing. I don't even know how long I'll be gone for. Once I'm there, I'll get a better idea."

Gina stopped her. "What about your publisher? Don't you have a deadline?"

"She said my next romance novel can wait. But I might be able to work overseas, depending on how I feel."

She briefly focused on the flowers again and then headed to her bedroom, remembering how her great aunt had always been there for her. Whenever she fell off her bike or got into fights with other children, Maria would disinfect the graze and stick a band-aid on her wound. She'd kiss it better, telling her, "You are all fixed now, my dear Rose."

Why was it so hard to move on? She thought she'd be feeling better after two weeks, but the pain in her heart still sucked her into flashbacks of her great aunt's smile, warm green eyes, and long hugs. Her aunt's death reminded her of the death of her father when she was only twenty years of age. She'd loved him dearly and wished he was here now to make her feel safe again. But no, she had to get on with things.

Fighting back tears, she squared her shoulders and pulled out her suitcase.

CHAPTER 2

G ianni Abbate blew on his frothy cappuccino as he sat outside a Pienza café with his friend, Sergio.

The warm breeze brushed his cheeks and crowds wandered around them. He squinted in the glaring sunlight as he pondered his next project.

"Here's last quarter's profits from the vineyard, Gianni," said Sergio, picking up the folder. He squinted. "But why are you getting involved in the family vineyard? What about your property development business? That's what's made you a billionaire, my man."

Gianni pushed back the ache in his chest as he took the file. "I know he probably didn't mention this to you, but I recently found out that my father has cancer, an aggressive one. He's dying, Sergio." Despite being outside, he undid two buttons that seemed to be choking him. It didn't help and he struggled to breathe evenly. *Get a grip, Gianni.*

Sergio's expression darkened. "Jesus. I am so sorry, man. Your father didn't tell me he was sick." He lowered his head. "But he hasn't been himself lately. Even the other day, he got dizzy inside the cellar. How are you doing, Gianni?"

He shrugged. squeezing his hands between his legs. "I have to be fine, don't I?" He pushed aside his grief. "I need to get on with things and help you guys out." He opened up the folder and stared at the numbers, barely registering what they meant. "How did it get this bad? The profits have plummeted. Why didn't you tell me? Surely, you had an idea."

Sergio shook his head. "I didn't. Your father put me on other duties for the past few months, telling me he had the finances handled."

Gianni's chest burned. "Are you serious? You're the damn accountant. You should've been on top of this. It's your job to know the numbers."

"You're right. I should've been. But after your father fired Julio, I became his replacement. I am sorry, man, but I had no idea it got so bad. Obviously, with his failing health, he must have forgotten to pay suppliers, but I'll fix it."

Gianni scoffed. "How? We've burned our bridges with the suppliers and now we'll need to develop relationships with new ones. We don't have the damn time to make new relationships when we're going to struggle with selling the next harvest." He slouched. "As if I don't have enough problems with this damn villa now."

"We'll find a way, man. You're grieving and can't see straight, but we'll sort it."

Gianni knew he was being hard on his friend when it wasn't his fault. It was his father who hadn't bothered to tell him he was sick, instead choosing to hide the truth from his family. Was it to maintain his sense of control, his need to feign his strength and hide his vulnerability? He was never a man to express his feelings and had shown that throughout his childhood. Like the time Gianni's father had brushed him off when he'd received a high mark on a science project or when he'd told him to 'suck it up' after grazing his knee during a bike ride. Then there was the time he'd lost a friend to suicide in high school. His father had said, "Just get over it already. Be a man." Oh, yes, his father was challenging to say the least, and it had always caused him pain.

Pushing his thoughts aside, he cleared his throat. "I'm sorry. It's not your fault. We'll figure something out." They might lose the vineyard if sales didn't pick up. His father hated how Gianni barely got involved with the vineyard, but it was a high-maintenance business with little reward. He wasn't sure he could increase profits.

Besides, he had another matter to attend to. "You know about the set of apartments my father's friend, Alfonzo, wants to build?" Sergio nodded. "Apparently the owner of that villa is coming from Australia. Her name is Rose and she'll be visiting here next week. I need to convince her to sell."

Sergio winked at a pretty woman walking by. "Right. So, you can build a set of three apartments on the block?"

Gianni nodded. "The house is old and hasn't been renovated in years, so Alfonzo wants to gift these apartments to his three children." He pushed aside his headache. "If any of the children decide not to live there, they can always rent them out and turn a nice profit." The pressure to get this villa had been mounting.

"What if she turns you down, man?"

"She won't. I'll convince her somehow, but then again, you're the ladies man. Maybe I should get you to talk to her for me?"

"Is she pretty?"

Gianni shrugged. "Haven't a clue, but I've sworn off women; I need to focus on work. They're more trouble than they're worth. ." His friend was a player and changed his girlfriends as quickly as his underwear.

"If you say so, man."

Gianni never got anyone to do his dirty work, and his father wanted him to sort out this business deal. He sighed. "No, it's my responsibility, Sergio. You can help me out with the vineyard. I feel bad not helping out as much as I should have. But with my primary work, there's hardly any time." As much as he'd loved Sergio since they first became childhood friends, he'd never liked the way he treated women. As if they were playthings. Rather, Gianni liked to wine and dine women, appreciating them like a fine vintage. The only problem was, he could never last longer than six months with any one woman. He found they always either tried to control him or kept secrets just like his father had all his life. Most had even loved his money more than him.

Subconsciously, he'd sabotaged those relationships. His last girlfriend, Lucia, had broken up with him because she'd found someone else. He was totally in love with her until he wasn't. It had been gut-wrenching when she'd told him about being in love with another man. She had initially enjoyed accompanying him to business meetings and long boat parties for property development contracts. But things had slowly died, and despite loving her, something in the relationship had been missing: They'd lacked a true connection. If she had been honest about how she truly felt, he could've changed things...

But no, she was yet another person who kept things to herself. He no longer trusted women, so it was best he keep to the single life. Women and Gianni didn't mix and relationships weren't worth the pain.

He returned the folder to Sergio. "I'm going to the boat. I need to chill and let go of all this. The water might give me clarity and help me sort out everything that's going on up here." He pointed to his temple.

"I can come with you, if you'd like," said Sergio.

"No. Thanks. I just need to be on my own. I appreciate the thought." He placed a few Euros on the table and walked away, his head down as he made his way to his car.

CHAPTER 3

Rose opened the passenger door of the taxi and brushed the sweat from her face, the humidity hitting her like a tornado. She walked behind the car and hefted her large overnight bag while the young driver pushed the suitcase towards her, nodding in her direction. "Thank you." The aroma of freshly brewed coffee mingled with the hot smell of engines permeated the air around her as she failed to wheel her suitcase with ease. The cobblestone street with its crevices and uneven surface made it impossible for her to push her luggage. She was dripping like a tap.

Waiting for the driver to leave, her eyes darted further ahead to the small strips of shops, crowds bustling about, and weathered apartments in shades of cream, beige, and brown. Wine stores stocked shelves of assorted wines outside and small groups of people entered them. The cafes looked inviting.

She dragged the suitcase with her overnight bag balanced on top of it and gripped her handbag tight as she heaved, wishing she was already at the villa without having to cart her belongings around first. The real estate agent was meeting her at this café here in Montepulciano before she moved into the villa. They had seen each other on Skype, and the villa was only ten minutes from the centre. At least he promised to drive her to the villa afterwards.

With a parched throat, Rose leaned forward, almost tripping over her suitcase when strong arms pulled her upright.

"Are you all right?"

She turned to her side and gasped. *Holy hell!* Where did this beautiful specimen come from? The man flicked back his short, wavy, light brown hair featuring blonde highlights, and found herself drawn into his sea-blue eyes. Stubble over his chin and around his mouth enhanced his looks. His well-toned, muscled physique incited tingles in her chest. "Yeah, fine. Thanks."

"Let me push this for you. Where would you like to go?"

She pointed to the café ahead with its cast iron chairs and square rickety tables underneath white umbrellas. Clay pots of brush were placed outside the café, but she couldn't see Guido, the agent, anywhere. Where was he? She took a seat at a table while her rescuer sat opposite.

She didn't mind him joining her. It should be a crime to be that good-looking.

"Are you here on holiday?" he asked.

"Not exactly. I'm here visiting my old place. I lived here many years ago, and so many memories are coming back. It's still a magical town."

He nodded. "Oh, the best. I never tire of visiting the wine regions and beautiful countryside. I couldn't imagine living anywhere else." His hands fidgeted. "Where is this place you're staying at? I don't mind helping you carry your luggage."

A waiter with a moustache approached. "What can I get you?"

She leaned back. "I'll have a limoncello please." He turned to Mr. Beautiful, who shook his head. Those searing blue eyes caused a flutter in her stomach and her hands dripped even more with sweat. It was so hot here. "It's only ten minutes away." Given that she would most likely never see this man again, he appeared easy-going enough for her to share what was in her heart. "My great aunt recently died and..." She pushed back tears. "I inherited the old villa I lived in years ago. It's a special place and I can't imagine what it will feel like once I arrive. Amazing memories. It's sentimental, you know?" She squared her shoulders. "I can't believe these developers think it's okay to tear down a house of history and beauty. Sharks."

He averted his eyes. "I understand." He cleared his throat. "Are you meeting someone here?"

"Yes. The agent. He should be here soon."

A fleeting darkness flashed in his eyes as he leaned forward and put out his hand. "I'm Gianni. And you are?"

She smiled. "Rose." The waiter returned with her bottle of limoncello and a glass and poured. "Do you live close by?"

"In Val d'Orcia, near Pienza, city of Siena. It's only twenty minutes away, but I love to come to the centre and catch up with friends. I enjoy the assorted wines here."

"Hmm. I don't mind wine, but I do prefer the sweet ones. They're hard to come by here in Montepulciano. I might have to change my tastebuds." She angled her head. "What do you do in this amazing country?"

He nodded, shuffling his feet on the ground. "I'm part of the family business. We own a vineyard here in Montepulciano." He handed her a business card. "If ever you want wine, drop in." He beamed. "Anyway, I had better leave you with your agent. It was a pleasure meeting you, Rose."

She hid her disappointment. The way he walked in his tight shorts and white fitted linen shirt caused her stomach to flutter. If there was a God, she might bump into him again. Would visiting Val d'Orcia near Pienza be on her agenda? But no. Was she mad? She wasn't here for romance but rather a mission concerning the villa. A quick review of the place then she'd be back on a plane getting on with her life.

Rose picked up the business card and read it. *Abbate Wines*. The address was listed underneath, so could she visit? She wouldn't mind buying some wine while she was here. It would only be a friendly visit.

Ten minutes after he left, Guido arrived. He was a young, handsome man with a slight paunch, a big smile, and friendly eyes. He waved. "Hello, Rose. Good to see you in person." Shaking hands, she grinned as passers-by gazed in her direction, possibly noticing she was a tourist. "Let's have a quick drink, then I'll drive you to the villa. You must be tired and jet-lagged."

Rose stepped out of Guido's car, her heart opening up to the beauty of the villa with its classic red brick façade, fenced front garden, and double-entrance gate. It was a two-story home with a balcony and window shutters.

Overhanging trees at the front and side of the villa gave it a rustic feel, and the uncut, dried grass needed tidying up.

"Does it still look good to you?" asked Guido.

Rose's heart soared with a warm smile. "It's weathered well over the past ten years, at least from the outside." He carried her suitcase as they entered from the front gate and inside the villa. A floral settee with lace cushions leaned against the wall on tiled flooring, and a set of stairs led to the second floor.

They walked upstairs, peering at the flowered quilt over a double bed, and admired an old armoire. Beside it stood a low, solid timber trunk which had stored the Manchester her mother had bought for her many years ago. An antique padded chair near the lace curtained window looked worn out, and paintings of Mother Mary and landscapes hung on the walls.

Guido set the suitcase by the bed, and she put down her bags. "As you would recall, there are five bedrooms and nine rooms. The villa needs some repairs, but the property developer's willing to do that himself at a lowered selling price." He huffed. "He will meet with you in a few days, so settle in, and let him know what you decide. But I must warn you. He is adamant to buy."

"I don't know yet, Guido. We'll see." Rose squeezed her hands, flooded with memories of how Maria had tucked her in bed with a stuffed toy by her side. How could she sell this villa when it held so much sentimental value for her? But then again, what would she accomplish by holding on to it?

She would settle in and make an informed decision based on their proposal.

CHAPTER 4

G ianni sighed, peering at his father, who pulled back the quilt while resting in bed. "Your doctor said you need to rest this week to get your strength back. You are in no shape to go to work. I'll take care of things." Why was his father this stubborn?

His father, Matteo, scoffed while ruffling his dishevelled curly black hair. His dark eyes penetrated Gianni's as if he could see through his son's soul. "I need to order those new wood barrels and talk to a few suppliers. Not to mention—"

Gianni put up a hand and pushed his father back into bed, but his father shoved him back. "Please listen. I will take care of all of that. If you don't rest, you'll end up in hospital. Is that what you want?"

His father shook his head. "Damn it, Gianni. You need to make sure that woman, Rose, sells the villa. I owe it to Alfonzo. He's been my best friend since we were kids and he's done so much for me. He needs those apartments for his children. Don't let me down."

Gianni swallowed, knowing he had to fulfil his father's wishes, particularly if he was dying. But how easy would it be? "I might get Sergio to talk to her."

His father put up a hand. "Whatever. Just get it done. No excuses."

Gianni couldn't believe he had met Rose before officially talking to her about the villa. The way she spoke about her old home made him sick to his stomach. The home held sentimental value for her, so he couldn't bring himself to tell her he was the property developer wanting to make the proposal to sell. She'd get a great price for it, but what if she wouldn't sell? Where did that leave him? No, he couldn't disappoint his father, especially since he had limited time available. It would most likely be his dying wish. He had to find a way to convince her. But if he told her who he really was, would she hate him for not telling her the truth to begin with? Then again, why did he care? She was a stranger. "When's Mum getting back?"

"Soon, I hope." He lifted his pillows and rested them behind his back. His father picked up his phone from the bedside cabinet and made a call.

While sitting with his father, who yelled at a supplier, Gianni scrolled through his phone. An image of Rose flashed back into his head. Her kind hazel eyes and glossy, long, strawberry blonde hair made her look like she could be on the cover of a magazine. He wanted to glide his fingers over the dimples in her cheeks. Even the tattoos of a rose and a sword on each shoulder made him sweat with desire. *Oh, stop it! Get a grip.* He wasn't in a place for romantic thoughts about a strange woman he'd just met. His mission was to help his father out in the vineyard and to sell Rose's villa to fulfil his father's wishes. He couldn't let him down.

Once his father had ended the call, Gianni said, "If Rose decides not to sell, then I'll find another location for Alfonzo. If it's a matter of finance, I'd be happy to fund it. He can pay me later. I can afford it."

His father squinted. "No, he wants that area. Nothing else will do."

"I can try to make it happen, but if it doesn't, I'm good at accomplishing things, Dad. I can find an area he'd like just as much. Trust me."

His father sighed. "You know...if it wasn't for the strong Abbate name, you wouldn't have succeeded in property development. I gave you the backing when you first started in the business. It's because of me you are a success. Remember that."

Gianni's chest constricted. His legs felt like jelly. "I'll be in the other room if you need me." He walked away with an aching heart.

Curiosity got the better of him when he strode into the lounge. He sat at a desk and clicked into his laptop, searching on the Internet for Rose Terrini. Inspecting the search results, he spotted several best-selling awards she'd won for her books, as well as positive reviews she'd garnered for her teaching work. One article explained how Rose had been inspired to write about romance when her great aunt had won and lost the love of her life. She had written a story which showcased Maria's story as a fictional narrative and she'd dedicated the book to her. Another article explained the loss of her father and how he had inspired her to achieve her ambitions while working in the publishing business as an editor and manager.

Rose had achieved plenty and had helped others write, inspiring people with her heart-warming stories.

Later that day, Gianni dipped his feet into his pool while skimming through a document outlining the contract of sale for Rose. The meeting would be in a few days, so he needed to get ready. Would it surprise her that he was the one organising this new development?

How could he possibly tell her he was the property developer wanting to demolish her villa when her exact words were: '*I can't imagine these developers thinking it's okay to tear down a house of history and beauty. Sharks.*' There'd been no chance for her to get to know him. Not that anything serious could happen between them.

He got respite in his home, a stone farmhouse with breathtaking views over the city of Val d'Orcia, and often enjoyed having friends and family stay over. It was a large enough home as he loved his space and enjoyed some isolation for balance between his busy lifestyle and the quiet.

Turning, Sergio walked towards him, carrying a glass of Chianti. He put it down beside his friend. "Are you nervous about this offer?"

Gianni put down the papers and grabbed his drink, taking a sip. The dryness of the wine relaxed him. "I met her yesterday."

He tilted his head. "Who?"

"Rose." He explained their encounter at the café. "I don't think she'll sell, but my dad's pushing for it. What if I can't convince her?"

Sergio sat beside him and submerged his legs in the water while gripping his wine glass. "So, you're telling me you realized who she was and said nothing?"

Gianni felt a headache coming on. "She was so sentimental about the place, I felt bad. I didn't think she'd want to sell. Maybe there's another way."

"What way? This is what your father wants, and you know how he gets. He won't let up until he gets what he wants."

"That's what scares me."

Sergio splashed with his feet and downed his drink in one go. "Your problem is that you're too nice to women. You let them walk over you, just like your last girlfriend."

He shook his head. "She met someone else, Sergio, and wasn't happy. I can't blame her when I was always busy with work. That's probably why she found someone else. I can't fault her for leaving."

"Hmm. You sabotage your relationships, man. All because you get too invested in the idea of love. You thought you loved your last three ex-girlfriends."

He shrugged. "In the beginning, yes, but I'm a man who craves love and finds women enchanting. Nothing wrong with that." He exhaled. "At least I know how to treat them with respect. You should learn the same, Sergio." Any relationship was always exciting at the start, and no doubt Rose's beauty captured him because she was new to the country. Nothing more, nothing less.

Sergio ignored the comment. "Let me talk to Rose. I can at least be objective. I'm a good salesman."

He shook his head. "No, it's my job to convince her, and I will."

Sergio put up his hand. "Up to you, man."

Gianni was not the type to deceive a woman, but it wouldn't be like that. He could have his friend talk on his behalf, but then again, he still had a few days to think about his strategy. All he knew was that he had to get her on side, and Sergio could be less biased than him, especially after he'd met her.

CHAPTER 5

The sound of a car horn alerted Rose to Luna, her childhood friend who still lived in Montepulciano. Luckily, over the past ten years, they'd kept in touch and knew about each other's lives. She grabbed her belongings and met her outside. She planned to hire a car in the next few days so she wouldn't be relying on Luna to drive her around.

Her friend was short and petite with rich brown eyes and red shoulder-length hair that fell in tight spirals. "Luna. It's been too long. How have you been?" She stepped inside the car and wrapped her arms around her, remembering the mischief they had got up to as children.

Luna's eyes glistened as she fell into the embrace. "Oh, Rose, so great to see you, cutie. You haven't changed one bit. Still as troublesome as ever, I see." Pulling away, she angled her head. "I have missed you so much, girl. What have you been up to?

"Oh, not much more since the last time we spoke. Same old job, same old friends, and about to make the biggest decision of my life."

"I hear you, Rose. But I admire you coming all this way to honour your dear aunt." She gave her a reassuring smile.

"That's the plan." Rose put on her seatbelt.

Luna started the ignition. "What's special about this winery?"

"Nothing. I wanted to do a bit of sightseeing, that's all. Now drive." Her friend sped all the way to Abbate Wines. Rose's eyes widened as she gripped the edge of the car seat, closing her eyes. "Slow down." Her friend obliged. "I'm surprised you haven't heard of this winery."

Luna turned to her. "I've never particularly liked wine and, as you know, I've been busy with nursing work overseas for the last few years. I just got back a few weeks ago."

Rose nodded. "Just in time to be together."

She hid her disappointment, having hoped that if her friend knew of the winery, she might've been able to get juicy details about Gianni. Was he single and how long had he worked at Abbate Wines? Would he mind her dropping in to buy a few bottles of wine? She was only visiting as she had the time and wanted gifts for herself and her friends. Nothing more to it.

She sat back in her seat, gazing through the window at the rolling hills, dips, and hues of varied shades of greens and browns against the backdrop of the blue sky. The bumpy ride over gravel and loose stones, and the drive underneath the shade of drooping trees led them to the Montalcino winery, which took just over half an hour. Her friend parked beside the winery, and Rose stepped out, smelling the freshness of the plantation, dust and debris as the scorching sun warmed her skin, making her squint.

Walking on to square concrete tiles, she admired the potted plants surrounding the place and padded chairs alongside the low brick fence near the entrance. Crimson roses in clay pots and herbs lined the front. The greenery gave it a cosy feel. The stone building was a grand presence as she ambled inside with Luna.

Making her way across the coloured slate tiles, she spotted photos of bottled wines and food hanging on the walls. White tables and brown padded chairs were placed haphazardly. The bare windows with drawn curtains cast a soft light inside. A woman was lining up bottles of wine on the front counter with empty wine glasses nearby. Shelves of wine bottles were set around the room.

Her heart pounded when Gianni approached, his eyes lighting up. He wore figure-hugging black shorts and a tight blue polo shirt. "You came. Welcome, Rose."

He remembered her name. "Hi." Her vocal cords felt knotted.

Luna put out her hand, and he shook it. "I'm Luna. An old friend of Rose's. Great to meet you. Nice place you have here."

He grinned. "Thank you, Luna." His eyes quickly returned to Rose. "Can I give you the grand tour?"

Rose ignored her parched throat. "Of course." They followed him to the other end of the room, and he led on to the wine cellar. The sudden chill in the air made her tremble while Luna made small talk with Gianni, who could not get a word in. Steel vats lined the space, as well as oak barrels.

"These are the French oak barrels which give the wine a stronger flavour, harvested in September. The fermentation process takes anywhere from one to five years and the wine remains in the bottles for four months. We have the DOCG and DOC status, which tells you it's a quality wine."

Rose was aware of how close he was, a hint of a woody cologne making her a little dizzy. "What grapes do you use?"

"We use the Sangiovese grapes, and also the Pinot Noir grapes. Half of each."

"Why do you have different barrels here?" asked Luna.

Gianni continued to look at Rose while he answered. "Different wood barrels give the wine a different flavour." His shoulder brushed against Rose's and his face reddened. Was he embarrassed by that? Get a hold of yourself, Rose. *Focus.* "It is a delicate process that creates mass production in these vats. We get at least 10,000 litres in each container. In the barrels, we can get at least 3,000 bottles."

"That's amazing," said Rose. "You obviously know a lot about wines, and I cannot wait to taste them. I am going to learn to appreciate dry wines." Admittedly, she wanted to taste him too.

"Hmm," he said, and their eyes locked until Luna interrupted the moment.

"I noticed olive trees on the way. How many do you have?"

"We have about five hundred trees, but we get them pressed by an expert. We don't have time to do it ourselves."

Rose nodded. "How long have you had the business?"

"It's been in the family since I was about five, so a long time. At least twenty-five years." That made him about thirty-years-old, but he looked younger. She listened as he continued to discuss the wine-making process for the next ten minutes, and then guided them back into the front entrance. "How about lunch? We can organise for you to taste four different wines with your meal, then you can decide if you wish to purchase any.'

"Sounds great," said Rose.

"Take a seat." Gianni set out four wine glasses for each of them and then filled their water glasses from a jug. "We have a set menu for our wine-tasting, with the food complimenting each particular wine you taste." He handed them menus. "The food firstly includes the Panzanella, which is an Italian tomato and bread salad, followed by Pici pasta, famous in Tuscany. Then we will serve you bread with home-made olive oil, and a chocolate and nut biscotti for dessert."

Rose licked her lips, salivating at not only the food. "I love Italian food. When I return to Melbourne, I'll have to make more of it."

"Yes, you need to stick to your roots. You mentioned living here, so I assume you were born in Montepulciano?"

"Yes. I grew up in Tuscany until I was eighteen. My parents thought I'd have better opportunities in Australia."

"Right. And what do you do?"

"I'm an author but I did work for a publishing house as an editor. I prefer working for myself. Sometimes I teach writing, too. When I'm needed." She remembered one of her writer colleagues, Grace, was teaching a writing course next week in Montepulciano. If only she had known months ago that she'd be here, then maybe she could've taught the class.

His eyes stared. "Wow. An author. I must look up your books. What genre do you write in?" Gianni leaned forward, his eyes fixating on hers as he licked his lips. Was he as attracted to her as she was to him? No, this couldn't happen. Be in control.

"Romance." She looked at Luna, who cupped a hand underneath her chin with a mischievous smile.

Luna whispered in her ear as their eyes locked. "I think you two should have lunch. I can wait in the car. You guys have it bad."

Rose blushed, hoping he hadn't heard her. She sighed, realising that her friend hadn't changed. Always saying the first thing that popped into her head. "We'll have our meals now."

Gianni swallowed and scratched at the base of his throat. "Of course."

Rose's shoulders deflated, heat still rushing to her cheeks as she bowed her head down in shame. She wouldn't get caught up with a man, not wanting to put herself through that pain again, especially when Hugh had explained how he'd never wanted a commitment. That he loved her but didn't believe in exclusivity when she'd found out he had another girlfriend. How could she ever feel safe with a man after that? It was the same emptiness she'd felt when her father had died. That same instability and loss she'd been feeling since losing Maria, not having had the chance to see her again.

Why would she get close to anyone again?

CHAPTER 6

R ose turned to Luna. "Why would you say that?"

Luna leaned forward. "Anyone who isn't blind can see the steam coming out of your ears. He likes you and I can see you're attracted to him too. Don't deny it."

Rose scoffed. "I love you, Luna, but you could show more tact. My friends say I'm bad with my loud mouth, but you're much worse than me."

Luna put up a hand in protest. "Oh, come on, woman. I mean well, and love you too. Life is too short to deny what you truly feel. How long are you staying?"

She shrugged. "I'm staying for three weeks and hoping I don't have to extend it."

"I'll miss you when you leave. You should stay longer, and we can properly catch up. I'm staying here for now. Probably won't work overseas anymore. It's exhausting." She rubbed her hands together. "Have you decided whether or not you're going to sell the villa?"

"Not yet, but I am leaning more towards a no. The place is still in great condition and only needs minor repairs. Honestly, I don't know if I can part with it. So many memories, and for them to demolish such a beautiful place... It's unthinkable."

"I hear you, girl, but you still have a few weeks to decide. Meet with the developer and make an informed decision." She looked up. "Oh, here comes Mr. Delicious," she whispered.

He carried a tray and set down the bowls of Panzanella. Was it hot in here? "I will bring you the first wine to taste. Enjoy." He returned a minute later. "This is a type of Pinot Noir wine which matches perfectly with the salad." His gaze turned to Rose as she unbuttoned the top button of her blouse before gently pouring the wine into their glasses when he accidentally spilled it on the table. "Sorry." He left and returned with a cloth, wiping the table before continuing to pour Rose's wine. "Ah, yes, this is..."

Rose tuned out about the flavours in the wine, scrutinising the way his lips moved and how he squeezed his hands together as if he was nervous. His breathing appeared shallow too. "Thank you."

Gianni stepped into the kitchen as their chef stirred the pasta. He took deep breaths and stood in a quiet corner. *Holy hell!* What was wrong with him? He had never spilled wine before nor been tongue-tied, so why now? He was making a fool of himself in front of a beautiful woman who he wished to get to know. But he couldn't think about Rose in a romantic sense when she'd undoubtedly just be like all the other women who didn't understand him. Who only saw him as the billionaire who could make all their dreams come true.

Despite being attracted to—or even loving—those women, he had always lacked that deeper connection. It was never real or authentic and lacked substance.

It was a no-win situation when his focus had to be on Rose selling the villa. He had to show his father that he could do this for him. Who knew how much longer he had to live? Time wasn't on his side.

He overheard Rose telling her friend that she would be in Italy for three weeks, but was that enough time for him to convince her to sell the villa?

Once the pasta was ready, he carried the dishes back to Rose and Luna, his legs heavy for the short walk. Taking a deep breath, he plastered on a smile. "We have our Pici pasta and the second wine to taste. It's the Chianti classic with its range of flavours." His eyes fell on the long outline of her neck and the way she continually touched the base of her throat. Flashes of red showed around her neck. *Focus, man.* "The flavours of this wine include red cherry, raspberry, balsamic vinegar, leather, tobacco, and liquorice. You have varied ingredients which makes the perfect combination."

"Interesting," said Rose, who picked up the glass after he poured it perfectly. "Mmm. It's dry, but it's becoming an acquired taste. It's kind of light."

"Exactly. It's one of my favourites." He locked eyes with her until she broke contact and forked her pasta. "Enjoy."

Heading outside, he sat on a chair and breathed in the natural plant scents, savouring the searing heat and wind sweeping his cheeks. He pondered the meeting in a couple of days and still wasn't sure whether to tell her the truth about his principal work. How could he explain he was lying to her about his true identity? Would she be okay with it, or could he explain he wasn't aware she was the woman he was meeting?

His phone buzzed, and he retrieved it from his pocket. "Hi, Dad. What's up?"

"Please tell me you have a great business strategy to convince this woman to sell, or is Sergio going to speak to her on your behalf?"

His chest burned as he gripped the phone, feeling like hanging up on the man. Was he ever in a good mood? "Her name is not *woman*. It's Rose, and no, I don't have a strategy as such, and I'm not sure who's talking to her yet. Why?"

"I just got a call from Guido, who said he doesn't believe she wants to sell. All that crappy sentimental shit. Well, I won't have it. This is too important, and you need to fix it. Change her damn mind however you need to. Just do it." He ended the call and Gianni pressed his lips together, clenching his fists. He wanted to throw his damn phone away and kick the rocks beside him. Standing up, he kicked a few loose stones and wandered close to the cellar, pacing up and down the hilly ground as he took slow, deep breaths. He needed to have his head on straight before serving dessert and the next drink to taste.

Five minutes later, he smiled at Giovanna, who manned the counter for a couple who held glasses and sipped wine for tasting. She was a young woman with long, bright red hair.

"The chef said the dessert's ready."

"Thanks. I'll head back out. Are you good here?" He watched Rose laughing at something Luna said and loved the sound of it.

She nodded. "Of course. We've got a tour group coming in about an hour, so we'll be busy then. Are you all right?"

"Great." He wasn't in the mood for a group and wished he could leave and talk to Rose for the rest of the day. But he had to help when his father demanded it, or the world would end.

Grabbing the small plates from out back, he returned to the front and set them down. After giving his spiel on the wine and dessert, Luna rose.

"I need a cigarette. I'll be back in five to enjoy my dessert." Luna walked out with a cheeky grin on her face. What was that about?

Rose tasted the wine. "Wow. Nice, but I'm getting dizzy. Trying four types of wine will do that to me."

He laughed and sat in Luna's seat. "Are you all right? Here, drink more water." He poured a fresh glass, and she picked it up and drank. He was jealous of the glass. Those lips of hers looked full and red, and he wondered what she'd taste like.

"I'll be fine. At least I'm not driving."

He nodded. "How's your new villa coming along? Have you settled in okay?"

"I have. It's brought back a lot of memories and I... I don't know. I don't know what to do. I can't live here yet. I can't..."

"Can't what?"

She put up a hand. "Nothing. Never mind." She picked up the glass and downed the rest of her wine. Her hands shook.

"Rose, you can tell me. It might help to get it off your chest. What's on your mind?" He hated himself for not telling her the truth, but why would he want to ruin their new acquaintance? The last thing he wanted was to upset her when she looked so conflicted and was still grieving for her great aunt. Also, if he knew what was on her mind, he could decide on how to convince her to sell or make new memories.

"The agent said his property development company wants to buy the villa, but I love the place. It has history, memories, and is still in great condition. There are a few things to fix, but nothing major. My mum said it was my decision." Rose peered past him. "My great aunt was being hounded by developers for years, but in the end, she wasn't sure." She took a breath. "The stress they put her under."

Gianni's stomach turned. "I am sorry."

"All they think about is the bottom line. But it's part of Montepulciano's history, and my personal history too."

His head pounded. "Right. But if you're not planning to stay, then why not sell? You won't be here to live in it."

"I know, but...still. I can rent it out rather than tear it down. It means a lot to me, and it'll be like cutting out a piece of my heart."

Gianni was speechless. The way her eyes lit up, talking about the place and how she couldn't part with it. His chest burned and his hands sweated as he watched her peer past him. He decided. Sergio could give her the spiel as he'd be objective. He didn't know if he could convince her otherwise, especially given how she felt about developers. Sergio had a way with women. A gift of the gab. Besides, she would most likely resent him for not being open in the first place. She'd hate him for his role too.

Luna returned, so he got up. "I'm ready to taste the wine and dessert now." She scrutinised him. "Hey, Rose is a writer. Maybe she could do an article about this place, give it some love and promote it."

Rose blushed. "I don't know, Luna. I've got my hands full with everything else here."

Gianni realised it was a way he could see her again. "I would love that, Rose. No rush on it, but we would appreciate it. It'd increase brand exposure."

Rose squinted. "All right then. I'll call you and set up an interview within the next week."

"Great." He beamed. "Enjoy your dessert." He walked off with a spring in his step. If she decided not to sell the villa, he wouldn't need to see her again after three weeks, and she would never need to know he was a billionaire property developer. Luckily, he didn't have a public profile and kept his wealth private.

CHAPTER 7

R ose leaned back in her chair as she gripped her phone, staring at the screen. "Hey, lovely ladies. Missing me yet?"

"It's only been a few days since you left, so no," said Gina.

Dalia shoved her playfully and shook her head. "Oh, don't listen to her, Rose. Of course she misses you and so do I. How's the villa?"

Rose took a breath while moving the FaceTime display closer towards her. "I'm meeting with the property developer today and the agent who will offer a proposal for me to sell, but I doubt I'll let it go."

Gina nodded. "Do not let those business types force you into anything you don't want to do. Is the place in good condition?"

"It is actually. Only a few minor repairs but doesn't seem to be anything too expensive." She looked around the rustic kitchen with its solid timber cupboards, thin, floral drapes, and metal pots and pans hanging on shelved walls. "This villa has been in my family for generations, so how can I allow this beautiful place to be destroyed?"

"What have you done over the past few days there? Did you reminisce with your friend Luna?" Dalia said.

Rose smiled. "I did. We went to a vineyard for a wine-tasting lunch. It was amazing. The owner gave us a grand tour..." She couldn't help flashing back to those immersive blue eyes and square jaw she wanted to run her hands over.

Dalia laughed. "Hmm. I see now. You've met someone. I can see it in your eyes, Rose. Tell me about him. What's his name and are you going out?"

Rose scoffed. "Oh, just because you and Luca are so in love doesn't mean everyone else is."

Gina's expression hardened. "Rose, you know I wouldn't normally agree with you having a fling, but after what you've been through, it might be okay to have a little fun."

"I have no designs on anyone, nor any wish to get involved. He is cute, but I have no time for that when I have this villa to sort out. I plan to travel to a few places here in Tuscany, seeing as I may never return. I could rent out the villa."

"Would you consider staying there?" asked Dalia.

Rose angled her head, pondering. Could she stay in a place which was her second home, particularly having family who lived in the south of Italy? She would have the chance to see them if she did stay, as she doubted she'd have the time to travel to the south now. But why was she entertaining such an idea? "I don't think so. Once I get these few repairs done on the villa, I might rent it out. But I have a few weeks to plan it all." A knock on the door jolted her out of her conversation. "Listen, ladies. I have to go. The property developer's here."

"Ooh, good luck," said Dalia. "Just let go and have fun. No harm in a quick fling."

Rose ended the call, then headed to the front door. Guido was accompanied by a tall, lanky man with a slick, gelled, black crew cut and a well-cut suit, who had a stiff yet professional demeanour and wore a bright-red tie. Rose smiled at them. "Hello, Guido."

"Rose, this is Sergio on behalf of the property developer, who couldn't make it. He's assisting with the contract and is a commercial accountant."

"Pleased to meet you, Rose."

She shook his hand. "Come in."

The men pulled out chairs and set out documents on the table. Sergio opened up a manila folder.

"Can I get you anything to drink, gentlemen?" She stood with her hands by her sides, wondering why Sergio seemed so unfocused. He had been staring at a document for the last minute.

"Not for me," said Guido. He turned to his companion. "Sergio?"

He looked up and clenched his hands. "Sorry?" She repeated her question. "No thanks. I would much rather get down to business." He cleared his throat. "Here is the contract."

Rose knit her brows and scanned through the proposal, her eyes widening at the number of zeros in the price for sale. *Wow!* She could slow down on her book sales with this figure. "Where is the property developer? Why couldn't he come?"

Sergio hesitated and looked at Guido, who shrugged. "He is under the weather, but I can assure you you're getting a great deal with the sale. It's only going to cost you more in renovations and maintenance down the track. We want to spare you all of that, Ms Terrini. This offer of sale won't last long, so we'll need your decision soon."

"I don't know. This villa has been in my family for years and to think you're planning to tear it down for apartments... Destroying history and what is sentimental to me. A lot of great memories, so it is hard to part with."

"But you don't even live here. It will be a challenge to keep up with changing laws around ownership or landlord rules if you decide on that route."

"But, surely, there are other locations you could secure for a set of apartments. Why here? This villa is part of our history and belongs to my family."

"It is the perfect environment for the buyer's children. He wishes to gift these to them, and he won't budge on finding a new area. The structure of this house is sturdy, so there'll be part of it that can be altered rather than destroyed completely. We're going to add a swimming pool in the backyard and get rid of the large space, which is not necessary and will reduce maintenance. And we're going to add—"

She shook her head, knowing that the beautiful land would be taken up by too many buildings. Why couldn't the damn property developer show up too? Wasn't this all his idea? "I think I've heard enough. This meeting is over." What they wanted to do to the villa broke her heart, but then again, what did she expect from a greedy property developer who saw nothing but a gold mine?

Guido smiled. "I understand it is hard to part with your family home, but owning this villa will only create more problems for you in the long run, particularly when you need to handle issues from such a distance."

Sergio gave her another spiel about the sale price, the rising costs of home ownership, and zoning laws. "Please give it some thought. We will wait a few weeks until you return to Melbourne, or possibly longer." He swallowed. "Speak to a lawyer and get back to Guido."

Rose sighed, realising this was a big decision to make on the spot. "Can I speak to the property developer?"

Sergio's face reddened. "As I said, he's not well and it might take him a while to recover, so you can talk to Guido or myself. Here is my card, and you have Guido's number too. Please, take your time. You can do so much with that money, and not have to worry about future expenses and debts." He stood up and Guido followed.

"Thank you for coming," said Rose. "I'll give it some thought, but I doubt I'll change my mind."

He nodded. "It's been a pleasure," Sergio said, with a fleeting darkness in his eyes.

"We'll be in touch, Ms Terrini," said Guido.

Closing the door behind them, her shoulders deflated as she wondered if the villa would be more of a problem for her down the road. But how could she destroy memories and love?

Rose flashed back to when her father had pushed her gently on her back as she rode a bike along the edge of the road, her hair sweeping across her face. He watched her like a hawk as she wobbled and zig-zagged her way down the quiet street until her bike leaned over and she fell on her side. He rushed to her and picked her up then scanned her grazed knee. "It's all right, darling. We'll try again tomorrow. You're nearly there." He wrapped his arms around her and made her feel safe and warm.

If she had the villa demolished, it'd feel like destroying those memories.

CHAPTER 8

Rose took in the freshly cut grass as she walked along a curved concrete path with assorted greenery and potted plants to the sides of it. The double-story farmhouse was majestic with the low and high brush surrounding it, sporting window shutters on the second level that gave it a peaceful ambience.

Rose was here for her interview with Gianni and had arranged a rental car, struggling to manoeuvre her way along the typical country gravel road.

She rang the doorbell and waited a few minutes, her eyes darting around the vast and peaceful area. Smells of ferns and flowers filled her senses as Gianni swung open the door, his eyes lighting up at the sight of her. "Hello, Gianni."

He grinned. "Welcome to my humble abode, Rose. Come in."

Walking inside the home, she entered a living area with a beige three-seater sofa, covered by green and brown pillows arranged neatly in a row. Opposite was a glass coffee table and desk, complete with a tall white lamp and open laptop. "This is a beautiful home. Do you do your own cleaning?"

He laughed. "No, I have a maid. Who has the time?"

She smelled his musky cologne as he came near, her heart pounding at the way his eyes brightened when he smiled. This house suited him, but she wondered if he had a side business she didn't know about. "Spacious kitchen." It had a stovetop over a steel counter with brown timber cupboards, a wood fire oven, and a rustic dining table.

"I love this place," said Rose. "How big is this property?" The family winery business must have done well for him to afford such a majestic home.

"It's 2.5 hectares of land surrounding this property. But it's hard to maintain as you could imagine. The home is two hundred and fifty square metres, which is spread over two floors and the outbuilding is eighty square metres, also on two floors and made of exposed stone."

Rose's heart warmed at his passion for architecture.

They made their way closer to the entrance. "You know a lot about this place. About architecture too."

"I love buildings. This home has undergone professional renovation while preserving the typical features of Tuscan architecture. You've got stone walls, terracotta floors, and exposed beams." He stared at his hands. "Sorry, I don't mean to boast. I'll shut up now."

"It's fine, but wow. Interesting how you know so much about buildings and properties. Are you sure you're only in the wine business? You're not an architect, are you?"

He hesitated, averting his eyes. "No, not at all." He cleared his throat. "Let's head on outside and we can talk there."

She nodded, and they strolled through an open door with more potted plants lining the outdoor patio and a view of a swimming pool and umbrella in the distance. The sun shone brightly, casting shadows on the concrete floor, with shading near overhanging trees and a partial marquee. Her eyes roamed the rolling hills, the landscape shades of cream, brown, and dark green. Patches of white lay amidst tall, rich green cypress trees. "This is my perfect place to write."

"I imagine it would be." He pulled out a seat, and Rose sat on a cane chair while he sat opposite. "My maid was just cleaning in one of the rooms, but she'll bring us drinks soon."

Scents of ground coffee and spices mixed in with dust and earthy smells. Was the maid making coffee with spices? "Great."

A young woman with brown eyes and auburn hair tied in a low ponytail approached and grinned in their direction. "Hello, signor. I have refreshments."

"Thanks, Valeria. This is Rose, who'll be promoting the winery through her writer's blog. She lives in Melbourne. Hopefully it will bring in new customers to the winery, as it's been quiet lately."

Rose beamed. "Pleased to meet you, Valeria."

She nodded. "A pleasure." Valeria set down a tray of two expresso coffee cups, iced water, and a plate of panettone and brioche. "Enjoy your time here, Rose."

"I will. Thank you for this." After Valeria left, Rose pulled out a pen and notebook from her bag and scrutinised the way Gianni bit his bottom lip as he tapped fingers on the table. He picked up his coffee and drank before wiping his mouth with a napkin.

"What would you like to know about the vineyard?" he asked.

She imagined running her hands through his stubble, flicking his long, wavy fringe out of his face, and drowning herself in those penetrating blue eyes. The scorching, humid heat made her body dehydrate as she sipped her water and then downed most of it. Wiping her lips with the back of her hand led to Gianni's eyes moving to her lips. Swallowing, she said, "I've...ahh...researched a lot about the vineyard. You mentioned it's been in your family for twenty-five years, so what I'd like to know is more on the personal side. What does the vineyard mean to you, and what are your plans?

Gianni rubbed the glass as if pondering. "A lot to think about, Rose." He grabbed a piece of panettone and took a bite. "Let's see. I haven't always worked in the vineyard but I have done other jobs here and there. More recently, it's made me realise how much love and care goes into growing wine. It's about taking great care of our employees, who grow to love wine, thriving when using different parts of the vineyard, separating the soil for a mixture of wines. We make balsamic vinegar too. We want to create that personal touch, so we pride ourselves on shipping directly to buyers. Our target market mostly comes from the United States." His eyes peered into the distance. "I remember when I was about seven, my dad carried me on his back and picked one grape. He made me eat it to decide if it was ready. I can remember the sweetness and the juice running down my chin. It was his love of the land that got me excited until..."

"Until what?"

He shrugged. "His dream of building the vineyard made him busier, and I saw him less over the years. My mother too. But the business and the stressors that came with it hardened him."

Rose grabbed a brioche and picked at it, listening briefly to birds chirping and crickets croaking. She leaned back in her chair. "I'm sorry to hear that. But that is a beautiful memory, and one you should never forget. I imagine you have other memories with your dad?"

"A few." He downed the rest of his coffee and leaned in, locking his eyes on hers. "Why don't you tell me more about you?"

She shook her head. "We're here about you, not me. I'm the one writing the article, remember? You still haven't shared your future goals and how you feel about the vineyard now."

His phone buzzed. "Sorry, I have to take this." He got up and turned his back to her, saying, "I'm in the middle of something and will call you back." Silence. "Sure. I hear you. Fine."

When he turned back around, his expression was stern and his brow arched. What had changed with that phone call, and who was on the other end?

CHAPTER 9

Gianni's stomach turned, thinking he should tell Rose the truth about his true vocation. When he'd mentioned having other jobs, he had been close to telling her he was the property developer. But that phone call from Sergio stopped him. His friend explained how he should wait until Rose gave them her final decision about the home, as she might decide to sell. But why did he feel guilty? He barely knew the woman, and a part of him hoped she'd sell. Whatever she decided, she'd be gone soon, so what was the point of her getting to know him? He wasn't lying about being part of the wine business.

"About the vineyard," he said. "I love the taste and juice of the grapes, the harvest periods when I can no longer feel my fingers, and the joy of tasting a range of wines that compliment Italian cuisine. I even love the coldness of the cellars, which wakes me up early in the morning." He took a breath. "As for the future, who knows? You'd need to ask my father about that, Rose. But I assume he'll still want to sell directly to buyers rather than distribute to stores."

"Hmm. My father made his own wine back in Melbourne." Her eyes misted. "He loved the Tuscan wines when we lived here," she said, her eyes looking away. "The drier the better. He was the type who would tell me not to drink a particular wine because it didn't match the food. He knew his wines."

An ache in his throat and a slower heartbeat made him initially speechless. He gripped the glass and yearned to reach out to her with his hand but stopped himself. She appeared wistful. "It is a popular wine. Does he no longer make his own?"

Rose rubbed a tear down her cheek. "He passed away. When I was twenty. He made the wine until he got sick. Then he couldn't anymore." Her bottom lip trembled, her body frozen in place. A hand to her flushed throat suggested she was trying to keep it together.

Oh, how he wished he could ease her pain. She was young when he died, and he couldn't imagine losing a parent despite his own differences with his father. "I am sorry, Rose. But it is nice to have those memories to hold on to."

She gazed past him, nodding. "When I was little, he would sometimes let me help him make the wine. I loved stepping inside the bucket filled with black grapes, getting sticky feet. The texture felt like heaven against my bare skin." She chuckled. "He even let me pour the wine into bottles, but most of the time, I only managed to get it on the ground. We had fun making a mess." Her eyes lit up as she focused back on him.

His heart ached for her. "It sounds great to keep him close that way."

An awkward silence filled the space as she brushed another tear rolling down her cheek. She picked up the notepad, gripping it for dear life. Was it a way to ground herself? She squared her shoulders. "Enough about me. Tell me about your childhood."

He wasn't sure he wanted the focus on him, but she obviously needed the distraction. "I was a good helper with my dad too, as a child, but before I say more, I'd like to talk more about your family. How is your mother doing?"

Rose hesitated. "She's great. Healthy, thank God, and has her own group of friends, so she keeps herself busy. My mum still works."

"I'm surprised she didn't want to come to Tuscany with you."

"She wanted me to deal with the villa as coming here brings up a lot of sad memories with my dad, but also good ones. I'm sure she'll return in a few years."

"She hasn't returned since you left?"

Rose shook her head. "No, she's been busy with work, and then my dad getting sick. It was hard for a few years before he died."

He nodded. "If you don't mind me asking, how did he die?"

Rose hugged her body tight as if fighting a chill and peered at a bird perching on a rock. The sunlight made her squint. "He had Parkinson's Disease." She rolled her fingers around in her palm, fighting back tears. "I miss him every day and wish he could have come back here with me."

Gianni couldn't help himself; he lightly stroked her forearm, then quickly pulled away. What was wrong with him? He couldn't attach himself when she was leaving in a few weeks and he needed her to sell the villa. Objectivity was key in business.

He gave her an understanding nod. "Grief is the worst thing in life. I remember a close aunt of mine dying at a young age. She had Cystic Fibrosis."

Rose's eyes darkened. "I'm sorry. How old was she?"

"Only thirty-five."

"I know with medical advances, some people with CF live longer now. Hopefully, it'll no longer be a death sentence. I have heard of a few cases where some have lived until they were in their eighties."

"Hmm, but it's rare." He exhaled. "We are a morbid pair, aren't we? Talking about disease when we should be talking about positive things.

"You're right. Let's get back to the vineyard." Rose asked him three more questions and jotted down notes until Gianni changed the subject. "Tell me how it went with your villa and the agent. Have you decided to sell?"

Rose tilted her head to the side, as if curious. "I don't think I'm going to sell. Too many memories, and I love the place. The agent convinced me to take time to think it over, but I probably won't change my mind."

Gianni pinched the skin at his throat. "But if you don't sell, what do you plan to do with the villa? I assume you'll be returning to Melbourne?"

She nodded. "Yes, but with the villa, I wouldn't mind getting tenants organised. Guido, the agent, should be able to help with that."

His throat burned, thinking his dad would be furious. "I understand, but as time goes on, it's going to be a struggle to keep costs down. It's when things break, and you might need a new air conditioner or a new fridge or whatever else breaks down—doing that from far makes it doubly difficult."

Rose pressed her lips together. "I hear you, but the alternative is worse for me. I can't imagine that beautiful building being demolished and turned into something more modern. It's all about greed with developers. Besides, Tuscany is about history, and we need to maintain that as long as possible." She knit her brows. "I might even decide to use it as a writer's retreat or guesthouse."

He thought it was a good idea to have it as a guesthouse, but he needed her to sell it. It was his way of proving to his father that he could succeed in one of his deals when he had failed with previous ones. His father hadn't talked to him for months, and it had been hard to start his property business when he'd needed to borrow funds from his father. In the end, he got a loan, and no longer owed the bank. "Sounds interesting, but you need to make an informed decision and consider all the options."

"Why are you trying to convince me to sell, Gianni? It sounds personal."

He ran a jerky hand through his hair, sweat lining his scalp. "I'm sorry. It's the businessman in me. I look at things in black and white for business deals."

"I get it."

By avoiding her eyes, he tried to fight a headache and pushed on his temple. Despite hating to lie to her, he had a high stake in this villa. He couldn't let his father down when he was dying. It might be his last chance to have his father finally approve of him. Once Rose left, he wouldn't need to worry about her anymore. "Would you like another coffee?"

Rose smiled. "No thanks. I think I'd better get going." She got up. "I have everything I need. I'll get you to check the article before I add it to my blog. Then I'll post it on social media."

"Thanks, Rose." Something in him told him to stop her when he remembered an upcoming occasion. "Listen. There's a wine-tasting event in Montepulciano next week. Why don't you come and see what it's like? It'll be an experience."

Rose swallowed. "Text me the details and I'll let you know."

"Will do."

What was he doing? He was supposed to be keeping his distance and here he was, inviting her to an event.

CHAPTER 10

Rose and Luna made their way around a set of tables covered with white tablecloths that fell to the ground. The humid wind brushed the back of Rose's neck as she stepped on the uneven cobblestones. Assorted wines and ice buckets, promotional booklets, and vineyard names on stands filled the square in Montepulciano. At a separate table under a marquee, a woman handed out glasses for the vineyards, so that guests could taste and buy their wines.

People pushed past Rose as she headed to the area where Gianni was pouring wine for a young man and woman in front of him. He stood next to an attractive woman who leaned in towards Gianni after he'd poured wine for the guests. The woman touched his arm, laughed, and bantered with him. He looked up and his eyes found Rose, smiling. She couldn't be jealous, could she?

Rose and Luna listened to the soothing sounds of a jazz trio while people sat on concrete steps around the raised concrete platform. The trio played trumpet, bass, and drums.

The heat hit her hard as she fanned herself. "It is so hot. I need an ice cream."

Luna shook her head. "Not without saying hello to Gianni first. But he looks busy; I don't know why he invited you to this festival if he's not going to be able to spend any time with you."

Rose shrugged. "Let's sit on the steps. I'm sure Gianni will come over when he's free."

Luna moved and whispered in her ear. "You've got the hots for him, haven't you? You might as well use and abuse him before you leave, girl."

Rose touched the base of her throat, shaking her head. Why did Luna need to put that in her head when she and Gianni were still getting to know each other, and she would be leaving soon anyway? "I don't have the hots for him. No way," said Rose.

Luna smirked. "Sure. Regardless, please don't leave me. I'm getting used to you being here." She winked. "Besides, if you decide not to sell, you might need extra time to set up whatever it is you need to set up with the villa."

"You could be my wing woman and settle things."

"No can do. I'll most likely be busy with work, so don't rely on me, Rose." She gave her a cheeky grin, sounding unconvincing. "Oh, the hottie's coming over now."

"What?" Rose rubbed the back of her neck and unfastened the top button of her thin blouse. She soon scratched at her throat, her heart pounding so hard she thought she might die.

Gianni wore a navy-blue shirt and beige pants, making him look ripped and strong. The way his eyes quickly darted from her head down to her toes was sexy. Did he think she wouldn't notice? "Hello, ladies. Thanks for coming."

Her breathing accelerated, and she flicked her fringe out of her eye. The music stopped and a man wearing a shirt, tie, and black pants spoke into the microphone, talking about payment for wine tasting and complimentary gift bags.

"You look busy," said Rose.

He nodded. "Only for another hour, then I'm all yours." Their eyes locked and Rose blushed. The awkward silence between them made her swallow and calm her racing heart.

Luna watched with a huge grin splashed across her face. She shifted. "Listen, why don't I help the lady over there and you can be with Rose now? I know a fair bit about sucking up to customers, so I can take your place."

Gianni laughed. "You would do that?"

She nodded. "Of course. Happy to help two people who are obviously destined to be great friends, even if she might be leaving in a few weeks."

Gianni tilted his head. "Might?"

Rose shoved her on the shoulder. "Just go already."

Luna laughed. "You love me."

"Thank you," said Gianni, who made his way beside Rose on the steps, watching the jazz band play a new tune. He turned to her, brushing her thigh with his leg. She ignored the tingle. "Luna should seriously work in comedy. She's a riot." He watched Luna briefly introduce herself to others while waving her hands around.

"I know. I thought I was the carefree one back home with my friends, but she's worse than me. Much worse."

"How so?"

She rubbed her hands together. "My friend Dalia is nurturing and optimistic about things. She's a software developer and loves helping people. Then you've got Gina, who is more on the negative side. The realist. She's a data scientist. But she's been through a lot and I can understand her caution and mistrust. I'm the most carefree of the bunch."

"Right. As they say, opposites do attract, and I love the way you look at life in a positive way. You seem to extract all that life has to offer. Hell, you're a famous author and that's no easy feat when many authors struggle to sell even a few books."

Rose wanted to wrap her arms around this man but contained herself. She gazed into the distance, as if needing to recover from his beautiful words, ignoring the soft tingles in her hand and warm sensation down her spine. "Thanks, Gianni. It's been hard and constant work. I'm determined in life. But how are you so certain I do well with my books, or that I'm famous?"

He scratched his chin and bit his lips, redness lining his cheeks. "Just a guess. But they're great qualities, Rose." He turned back to Luna, who was pouring a glass of wine. "Have you tried any of the wines?"

A guess. Surely, he must have looked her up online. Her popularity wasn't a secret, so why couldn't he be honest with her about his interest? "No, we just got here." She pushed the idea out of her head, thinking that Gianni didn't want to give her a sense of hope in their relationship when there was none. The ache in her chest soon dulled. "How is business? Have you sold anything?"

"A few bottles; not so bad. We have a bit of competition, but we've also had bulk orders." He touched her shoulder.

"Thanks again for that article about the winery. I think you might have given us more visitors. It was a great profile. My father appreciates it too."

"My pleasure. I love writing, even if it's not fiction."

"Well, it shows. Amazing work." He beamed. "Why don't we grab an ice cream, then you can tell me all about your work." He pulled her up by the hand.

A flutter in her stomach made her wobbly on her legs. "Sure."

Rose walked beside Gianni as they passed by restaurants, a wine store, a souvenir shop, and a woman's boutique. Her sandals slipped in the heat as they strolled down the cobblestone streets. She gasped as she almost tripped on the slippery surface when Gianni pulled her by the hand.

"Are you all right?"

"I'm not used to walking this much, particularly in these sandals. I need better shoes that don't make me slip."

"We're here now." He stepped inside the ice cream shop and she followed. "What would you like?"

"I'd love a zabaglione."

He chuckled. "Funny. That's my favourite ice cream too." Gianni placed the order while Rose felt a wall of tourists and locals waiting behind her. Muffled voices and scents of body odour caused her to hold her breath.

A sweaty older man with grey hair moved beside her and licked his lips. "Hello, beautiful. You're not from around here, are you?" He spoke in Italian, and she pretended not to understand as she made her way towards the store exit. Gianni glared at the man as he bought their ice cream cones and handed her one. The man put up a hand as if to say sorry, then approached the counter.

As they headed outside she took a deep breath, thinking how some Italian men loved to flirt, even if he was old enough to be her father. "Good call there, pretending not to understand, but you speak Italian well, don't you?"

She angled her head then licked her ice cream, savouring the sweet brandy flavour. "I'm fluent, but I've lost some of the vocabulary." They made their way back to the square.

Gianni led her back to the steps as they listened to the band. "Oh, you've got ice cream on your lip."

She wiped her mouth. "Is it gone?"

He shook his head and leaned in, pressing a finger over her upper lip as he wiped off the ice cream. Clearing his throat, he said, "All gone."

"Thanks." She faced away from him, her heart racing a mile a minute. *Stop it!* She couldn't be attracted to the guy when she was about to leave. But the way he stared at her suggested he might be attracted to her too. She couldn't get her friends' fling idea out of her head. It wasn't like this was new to her when she'd had her fun in Melbourne, especially when she was looking to fill the emptiness in her heart.

No, Rose had to focus, to keep her emotions under lock and key so she could make the right decision about the villa. She couldn't get distracted by a gorgeous man who lived in another country, not to mention her grief affecting her ability to pursue anything more. They were better off as friends.

Her phone buzzed in her hand after she finished her ice cream. It was the co-ordinator of the university where she taught short writing courses. "Hey, Jude. What's up?"

"Listen, Rose. Seeing as you're in Tuscany, we were wondering if you could step in for Grace, who is supposed to be teaching a writing class in Montepulciano next week. She's sick. Can you take over?"

She could barely breathe. "What? But that's like an eight-week course. I'm leaving in two weeks." Gianni stared at her curiously as he licked his ice cream.

"I know, which is why we're offering to pay you not only for teaching, but for your expenses over that period. We are desperate. There is no-one else travelling to Tuscany, and if we don't fulfil this, then we'll have to refund the money. It'll be a nightmare. Please. They're from all over the world, and it's a great way to promote our overseas writing courses. Pretty please?"

She had a life in Melbourne and couldn't imagine staying here for that long. She'd miss her family and friends, but knew she had no tight deadlines with her publisher. Staying longer meant getting more attached to Gianni, didn't it? But this could be a way for her to do something she loved; helping others in her own passionate pursuit and success. "Fine. I'll do it. Send me the details and resources to my email address."

"Oh, thank you, thank you," said Jude before ending the call.

"Is everything all right?" asked Gianni.

"Depends on how you look at it." He looked at her strangely, then she stared at her hands, a rush of adrenaline hitting her at the idea of having more time with Gianni. No harm in just being friends, right?

CHAPTER 11

"Okay, students, today's topic is how we show and don't tell in books. Let me give you an example." She picked up her marker and wrote on the board: *Thomas told her he'd had enough of her cheating ways and walked out angrily.* "In your books, I'd like you to write this to show the action. Then share it with your partner and we'll write a few examples on the board."

Rose sat on a black, netted-backed chair at a table after her second day teaching the basic writing class for the university. Despite the holland blinds being mostly drawn down, the sunshine still filtered into the room, illuminating its beige-tiled flooring, rows of tables and chairs, and twenty-five eager beginning students, whose eyes lit up at the task set out.

The large room had a heater against the wall, three large bay windows beside the tables, a closed solid timber door, and a TV unit behind her. She loved teaching.

Loved seeing the fresh and energised students who were as passionate about writing as she was.

Loud voices grounded her as students in their twenties to forties bowed their heads over their notepads, scribbling down notes and turning to their partners to compare. Rose wandered around the room, nodding and smiling at the few people who'd already sat back and put their pens down.

"Okay, let me write a few of your examples on the board. Anyone care to share?" She grinned at a woman named Julie who came from the United States and had the brightest red hair with copper highlights. "What do you have?" She lifted her marker to the board.

She cleared her throat. "Thomas clenched his fists, glaring at her. 'I've had enough of your cheating ways.' He stormed out."

"Great. Let's have more examples." Hugh came to mind, causing her to think about just how much he had hurt her when he'd cheated. *Focus.*

At the end of the lesson, Rose sighed and grinned at the students as they picked up their bags and waved goodbye.

"See you next week, Rose. Love your class," said Julie.

"Thank you. See you then." She waved at the students, who exited through the open door as she stacked her folders and papers together. Opening up her satchel, she placed the resources inside and clipped it shut. The quiet in the room gave rise to thoughts about Gianni from last week. She hadn't heard from the guy for a whole five days and it was driving her crazy. She must have scared him off after telling him she was extending her trip by another two months due to the writing course. He obviously didn't care to babysit her for that period, but why worry? It wasn't like anything was going to happen, despite her dreaming of him every night and having him on her mind during the day. Surely, once she returned home he'd be a passing memory. But who was she trying to convince? Her heart ached and her sadness showed when no one was around. She was great at masking her genuine emotions. Would she ever see him again? Now that she'd written the article and toured the vineyard there was no reason to see him, and Gianni had said nothing last time.

Resting her arms on the table, she gripped her elbows and swallowed. An emptiness filled her like nothing else had. No man had ever made her feel this way. What was wrong with her? Nothing. She was only fantasising about a man because of the romantic setting of Tuscany. It was just that—a fantasy.

"Penny for your thoughts?"

Rose quickly lifted her shoulders and turned to the familiar voice. "Gianni? What are you doing here?"

He approached and stood opposite the table. "I just saw your students. Eager beavers who looked excited. They must love your writing class."

She nodded, rising, and grabbed her satchel. "They said they did. I love teaching as much as I love writing." Rose made her way alongside Gianni down two sets of stairs while holding onto the rail, concerned about her jelly legs. Their shoulders brushed, and he turned to her with bright eyes.

Once they reached ground level, they passed by an open area filled with grey stools at high-topped round tables, surrounded by photographs of Montepulciano's history hanging on the walls. As she walked through another door leading to an outdoor area where people sat on steps opposite a café, the heat hit her square in the face.

Gianni turned to Rose. "How about this café for dinner?"

"Sure. I could eat." Rose wondered what his game plan was and why he'd come to see her today. Did he feel obligated to ask her out because of the blog she wrote, or did he have romantic feelings for her? Not that they could do anything when she was here for one reason only: to make an important decision about the villa.

She pushed through the crowd, headed inside the coolness of the café and made her way to a table. The ambience was romantic in the low-lit space; a scented candle on the table and Italian music playing. It was one of Eros Ramazotti's old songs she loved called *Musica E*, reminding her of her ex-boyfriend from Tuscany. The ballad warmed her heart and led to her and Gianni staring at each other as he licked his lips, her body responding with a lightness and a fast heartbeat.

"Here are your menus. Can I get you drinks to start with?" said a handsome, burly waiter who held a notepad.

Rose gazed at the waiter, whose eyes lingered on her. "I will have...an iced limoncello."

"And I'll have your house beer." Gianni glared at the man, whose eyes were glued to Rose.

"Of course. I'll be back to take your order." He headed off to the back and turned to watch her again.

Gianni shook his head. "He looks like a sleaze."

"Why do you say that?" asked Rose. She touched the base of her throat, aware of his eyes fixed on her lips. Why was she aroused right now?

"It's obvious," he said without expanding on his comment.

Rose didn't press the issue, but glanced at the menu. Light-headedness and shuddering breaths caused her mind to go blank for a minute. Rose thought that Gianni might be attracted to her, but was fighting to keep himself neutral judging from the intermittent stares he gave her. The idea flooded her with warmth and her mouth moistened. She flashed back to the way his eyes had lit up then darkened after she explained her extended trip. "I'm going to have the antipasto."

He nodded. "Hmm. The ravioli with cream sauce for me."

The waiter returned a few minutes later with their drinks and kept staring at Rose. She looked away with heat rising across her neck. This guy was handsome, but he didn't compare to Gianni. She only had eyes for him. "Can I take your order?"

Gianni sat back, tilting his head. "Only if you stop staring at my girlfriend." The man said nothing but put up his hand as if to apologise.

Rose gasped, her face warming. "I'll have the antipasto, thank you."

After Gianni placed his order, the waiter nodded and avoided Rose's eyes. He rushed off as if he couldn't get out of there fast enough.

"Why would you say that?" asked Rose.

He shrugged. "It worked, didn't it?"

"I guess it did." She averted her eyes and sipped her limoncello, relishing the strong alcohol and sweet, lemony flavour. Why did her spirits lift at the idea of being his girlfriend? Each time she saw him, her feelings only grew stronger, and it scared the hell out of her. Why did he care if another man stared at her when they would never have claims on each other? He was giving her mixed signals.

CHAPTER 12

F orking his pasta, Gianni wondered why he was jealous of the waiter staring at Rose. His chest had ached and his body heated up at the idea of her looking at another man. It was crazy how infatuated he was with her. But then he thought about how he hadn't told her the truth about looking her up online. Why bother when he didn't want to give her the wrong idea, given they could never indulge in a relationship? Rose would be leaving the country soon. She'd be one more woman who wouldn't understand him or see the real Gianni behind the billionaire status. He knew he was more than his money.

He thought about his ex-girlfriend who had never got to know the authentic Gianni behind his wealth. He flashed back to how most of his girlfriends had never got to know him as a man of value, who had emotions and heart. A man who felt things deeply and wanted to be heard. All they saw was Gianni the property developer, or Gianni the man with the boat who loved to entertain. In the end, he didn't trust them, and on a subconscious level, likely pushed them away. Gianni wanted to trust women, and had the desire to move past his issues, but was he capable?

He didn't like how Rose was always on his mind. The way her dimples lifted when she smiled, and the curve of her neck that made him crazy with desire. He wanted to reach out and touch her. It was even in the way her eyes lit up when she talked about her writing, and the way she touched her rose tattoos when she was nervous.

"Is your father proud of the work you do at the winery?"

He drew out of his reverie, not knowing how to respond. "I'm sure he is, but he's not the emotional type. He's the 'just get it done' type of guy, but I love him."

"My dad was the complete opposite. He doted on me. My mum fought with him because he spoiled me rotten, especially when I acted out."

Gianni laughed. "I can see how you would've been rebellious. Do you have any siblings?"

"No, just me. But my two close friends, Dalia and Gina, are like my sisters. I miss them. Now that I'm spending more time in Italy, it's hard to be without them. I tell them everything."

"But you have your old friend, Luna, here. You two seem close."

"We are, but we haven't seen each other for ten years, so we have a bit of catching up to do. She's a lot of fun and got me into a lot of trouble when we were young at school. One time, she told a guy I had a crush on that I liked him. I was so embarrassed."

"What happened?"

"He asked me out and became my boyfriend. I was never shy around boys, but with this guy, it was different. He got me. Understood me."

Gianni's eyes darkened as he sipped his beer and put it down, part of it spilling on the table. He had no right to be jealous and pushed away the thought. He wiped it with a napkin. "How long were you together, and where is he now?"

Rose shrugged. "I don't know where he is, but he doesn't live here anymore. We were together for two years and then broke up because my family moved to Australia. It was hard, and we tried to keep the relationship going, but he eventually met someone else." She remembered being heartbroken after hearing the news from Luna.

"Long-distance relationships don't work," he said and a hint of hardness fell into her eyes. "You need to see each other to work on a relationship. You must've had other special men in your life?"

A fleeting sadness penetrated her gaze. "My last boyfriend hurt me a lot. Kept a secret from me." She pressed a hand against her chest. "I thought I'd die from heartache. But then I realised it wasn't meant to be. After that, I had a few casual flings with guys. Easier that way. No strings attached."

Gianni nodded. "It is hard to trust people. I get it." Rose avoided his eyes as if she battled with a thought. "Do you mind me asking what his secret was?"

Rose knit her brows and pressed her dainty hand underneath her well-shaped jaw. "He introduced me to a woman he said was his sister, but in truth, was his girlfriend."

Gianni lost his breath. "What?"

"Yeah. I'd seen him with this woman a few times around his work and home. I asked him about her, but he said she was his sister, visiting from interstate. I believed him. He was having a relationship with both of us at the same time. It hurt a lot because I loved him."

Gianni felt a need to pound into the bastard. How could anyone cheat on Rose? Beautiful Rose, who had the heart of an angel. He had never cheated on any woman and always showered them with care. "I am sorry. That must have been hard."

Rose clenched her hands, picking at a piece of pecorino cheese and washing it down with her drink. "Anyway, I guess it makes it hard to trust guys. They always have some sort of secret, which results in the loss of the relationship. I'm happy with my work, friends, and family. It's enough for me."

Hell! He was keeping a secret and hated himself right now. When she'd told him she was spending more time here, he'd panicked, thinking that he might have to tell her the truth. Would she understand how he had to keep this billionaire status a secret? If he told her the truth now, she'd hate him, especially because she despised wealthy people. But she'd leave soon, and he wouldn't have to deal with the possible fall-out. "If men have a secret, they usually keep it for good reason." Taking a breath, he explained. "Let's say you had a man lie about his resume and you're the owner of a company. But the reason he had to lie was to earn enough money to pay for an operation for a family member. There was no other job available, and he was desperate for this job. It was a matter of life and death because, without the operation, his family member wouldn't survive, and he needed the money in two months. Wouldn't that secret be justifiable?"

Rose scoffed. "Not the same. Depends on the case, Gianni. Please don't change this around to make it about a life and death situation. My ex lied out of a huge sexual appetite and cheated on both of us. His girlfriend thought *I* was his sister, so he lied to two people. There's no coming back from that."

"Rightly so, but what I am saying is that anyone can keep something from you for good reason. It's all I'm saying. Nothing is black and white."

Rose nodded. "Fine. I suppose that's true. But it's hard to trust that person even if the lie is justifiable. How would you feel about someone keeping a secret from you?"

"Hmm. I don't trust easily either, so it would be hard."

Rose chewed a piece of prosciutto. "You are the nice guy type, aren't you? Are you telling me your ex-girlfriends never kept secrets from you?"

He shook his head. "No, not that I know of. I'm Mr. Wonderful and women cannot resist me. Haven't you figured that out by now?"

Rose blushed. "Right. If you say so. Why don't you tell me about your last relationship? How special was it?"

He stared at his hands, then scratched his right palm in thought. It hurt him at the time, but he was over her now. "My ex-girlfriend left me. Thought we could have spent more time going out. We were together for over a year, and I loved her. When she left, it felt like fifty knives penetrating my chest. She met someone else, so that was the last straw. The pain was surreal." He later vowed never to fall for a woman again.

"I'm sorry. Do you believe that you never spent much time with her, or was that her perception?"

He shrugged. "I wasn't spending much time with her. It was partly my job, but I could've arranged things differently if I wanted to. I sabotaged the relationship because deep down, I couldn't trust her. She didn't appreciate me for me."

"Why didn't you break up with her rather than sabotage it that way? It's playing games, Gianni. Not being honest."

He drank his remaining beer. He realised that he hadn't been honest in most of his relationships. Was that a pattern with him? Did he struggle to be honest because he believed they wouldn't appreciate the true Gianni, the man rather than the billionaire? "I didn't think she'd listen to what I had to say and had made up her mind."

"But your feelings didn't change, did they?"

"No, they didn't." He grabbed a piece of bread and dripped olive oil over it, then bit into the soft, moist texture. He wanted to change the subject, not feeling great about himself. "This bread's amazing. You should try it."

Rose poured olive oil over her bread and took a bite. The way her coloured lips wrapped around the bread made him want her even more. Why couldn't he stop fantasising about her, wanting to taste the inside of her mouth? Telling her the truth now meant he would lose her friendship, and he didn't want that.

CHAPTER 13

G ianni had his phone on speaker with his friend, Guido, opposite him. His father's friend worked as an architect, and they often worked together. "Alfonzo, I'd like you to create those blueprints today. For all those farmhouses. Time is of the essence. The investors are getting itchy feet." He lay back in his ergonomic chair and tapped a pen on his solid oak desk.

Certificates of his business degree and property development training lined the walls to the side of the grand oval office, leaving space for a sofa and coffee facilities beside him. Landscape paintings hung on the wall, softening the corporate vibe.

Alfonzo replied. "One of those farmhouses needs a lot of restoration. Instead of turning it into a luxury villa, why don't you keep it as a quaint home and keep the same design? That way, we'll save on time."

"Not a bad idea. Okay, get it done. Thanks, Alfonzo." He ended the call and turned to Guido. "It's happening. We're set to build those luxury villas on about eighty hectares of land."

Guido lay his hand underneath his jaw, pondering. "Is the plan to build the golf course, swimming pool, and spa?"

Gianni nodded. "Not only that, but we're planning to set up apartments, artificial lakes, and commercial buildings. The rent alone for new businesses will be lucrative for us. We're even having a luxury boutique hotel and a retirement village. A grand project which will put us on the map, Guido."

"Sounds like it's happening," he said, his eyes darkening.

"Of course, it's not about the money but how we can help the Northern Tuscany community. It is creating jobs too. The unemployed will get work that'll last for many years. It's a monumental project." He could tell Guido had something on his mind. "What's wrong?"

"Listen, I'm your partner and friend, but I have to say this." He stared at his hands, then got up and turned to look out of the large window behind his desk. "What you're doing with Rose is questionable."

Gianni's breath slowed down, his face warming up. "What do you mean?"

He turned and sat back down with his hands clasped in his lap. "Why haven't you told Rose who you are? She deserves to know the truth."

Gianni scoffed. "And what? Turn her away from me? I thought she was leaving earlier and now that she's staying longer, I thought about telling her. But she'll hate me and I—"

"You have feelings for her, don't you?"

Gianni nodded. "I can't stop thinking about her, Guido." He pressed his hands into his chest. "I don't know what the hell I'm supposed to do about that. I don't want to lose her, but I don't see a future for us when she lives on the other side of the world."

"Is that why you haven't been honest? Because she's leaving?"

"Partly, but you're right. I have to tell her the truth."

Guido leaned back in his seat and then stood again. "Good. When are you seeing her next?"

Gianni rubbed his hands together, sick to his stomach about telling her the truth. Would she hate him? Or would she understand that he didn't want business to interfere with their friendship? "I don't know yet, but I'll need to take her to a special place. Set the right mood. Hopefully, once she realises that I care for her, she'll understand I didn't mean to lie to her."

"Make sure you do it before she finds out some other way. Like Sergio, for instance."

"He was the one who said not to say anything."

"Typical. But please don't take advice from a man who thinks wining and dining a special woman is to say, 'wham bam, thank you ma'am'. I love the guy, but when it comes to women, he has a lot to learn. Call her now."

"You're right." He flung a document into his in-tray and grabbed his phone.

Rose sat outside on her balcony typing on her laptop set on a small table breathing in the scents of pine, distant smoke, and blooming roses from her front garden. The sunlight warmed her face, and the light wind gave her a sense of peace. A panoramic view of the mountainous landscape made her think about how she'd love to wake up this way every day. But in less than two months, she'd be returning to Melbourne and Gianni would be a distant memory.

The tightness in her chest and heaviness in her body made her think twice about what it would be like to kiss him at least once. Why couldn't they enjoy each other while they could? They could have nearly two amazing months together.

Brushing aside her thoughts, Rose clicked keys to bring up images of a scene for her current romance novel in her mind, which had a three-month but flexible deadline from the publisher.

Rose had woken up that day with memories of the villa. She flashed back to the time her hands had shaken while opening a letter she'd been expecting. Her heart had stopped when she read that she'd won a writing competition. Her father's eyes had lit up as he patted her on the back. "You have a gift, Rose. Nurture that. I believe in you."

She'd swallowed as she turned to her father with pride. "I don't know, Dad. I just got lucky, that's all. It could've been anyone."

He shook his head firmly. "No, you listen to me, Rose. I have read your stories and they are amazing. I want you to follow your dreams, darling, and if writing is one of them, go for it." Her heart warmed at the way her father had appreciated her. She missed that. He had died way too young.

She also recalled the times she had learned to make Panettone with Maria as they made a mess and laughed together, getting flour all over her face.

Even the time her mother had hugged her all night after crying incessant tears from an argument with her boyfriend, which had made her feel safe and loved in the villa.

Tears formed in her eyes as her chest burned with an aching sense of loss for her father and great aunt. She realised that moving away from here had made her feel more isolated without his wise counsel and love. Maria's death had triggered those memories, but had also made her acutely miss her great aunt, who'd loved her unconditionally.

It was decided. Rose would not sell the villa. She didn't know what the next step would be, but she refused to have it destroyed. No, the villa was special and had to be preserved.

She grabbed the phone from her back pocket, about to call Guido, but then thought twice about it. No, she needed to go there and tell him in person. Do the right thing.

When her phone buzzed in her hand, she checked the display. Gianni? "Hi there."

"Rose, how are you?"

"Great. Just working on my romance novel, with a view to die for. How are you?"

"Good, good. Listen, I wanted to show you around Tuscany and thought we might take a trip to Montalcino and a few other places, like Florence and Pienza. You have to see more of Tuscany while you're here."

"It sounds great, but don't you need to work?"

"I can take a few days off. Would it work if I pick you up in about an hour?"

Her heart raced, her mind ruminating about what to wear. "Sounds good. See you then." She ended the call and squared her shoulders, a tingling in her fingers and dry mouth making her realise something. Could she get him out of her system, so she'd no longer wonder about him? Surely, fulfilling this ache in her heart would be worth spending one night with him, or even two. Had her friends been right about her needing a fling? No harm in that when they could fulfill their needs then move on.

CHAPTER 14

The beeping sound of the limousine horn must have woken up the neighbourhood as Gianni stood outside the back door, waiting for Rose to come out of the villa. His hands sweated, and his throat felt tight as he calmed his breathing. This had to be the day he told Rose who he was, but only after getting her in the right mood and explaining his need to hide his identity. She didn't need to know his billionaire status, just that he was the developer behind the sale of her villa.

Sounds of footsteps and the snap of a twig alerted him to her presence, causing his breath to slow. She was a vision in her loose-fitting singlet black dress, which fell down to her knees, its thick straps revealing the toned outline of her shoulders, proof that she worked out. Her flowing hair draped neatly over her bare arms. The feminine curve of her legs made him want to glide his fingers over them. *Focus, Gianni.*

Rose's eyes lit up. "What the hell is this, Gianni? A limousine?" She drew closer, and he kissed her on the cheek, lingering as the floral scents of soap and lavender permeated his senses.

"Why not? Let's indulge while you're here." A fleeting hint of darkness penetrated her eyes. "Take a seat, my lady."

Her smile was infectious. "Yes, sir." He held the door open for her.

Gianni sat beside her on the back seat. "This is Flavio, our driver for today."

"Hi, Flavio. Pleased to meet you."

The bulk of the man turned and nodded. "Pleasure is all mine," said the driver. "Our itinerary for today is a visit to Pienza, followed by a Montalcino winery for a cheese tasting picnic, then off to Florence for our final destination."

"Sounds amazing," said Rose, looking at Gianni. "This is all great research for one of my books. I visited none of these places when I lived here. It'll be an experience."

Gianni nodded. "Anyone who visits Tuscany must see these sights. Who knows when you'll return." A deep, empty pit filled his stomach, but he pushed it away. He could show her a great time and make special memories.

Rose stared out of the window, her eyes dilating at the panoramic views of Montepulciano as the limousine manoeuvred through the rough terrain around winding roads and gravel surfaces. Gianni never tired of the cypress trees, and the flat and uneven ground under the backdrop of the blue sky. "I remember driving to some of the smaller villages around Montepulciano. There's so many of them, they sometimes look the same."

"The same, but each has its own unique culture. Val D'orcia is my favourite because I live there. But Pienza's not too far away. Nothing like getting up to those breathtaking views."

Rose nodded. "Thanks, Gianni. I appreciate you taking me around."

Gianni beamed in silence, and when the limousine stopped, he stepped out of the vehicle and headed around to Rose. Their hands brushed, and he held onto the small of her back. "This is Pienza."

Rose's eyes squinted in the sun as she walked alongside Gianni with a set-up of marquees and market stalls. Her eyes darted to the other side, where there was an old building that housed a restaurant. People ate breakfast, and apartments featured window shutters and balconies above.

She felt unsteady in the heat as Gianni touched her shoulder while passing by a jewellery stall. Picking up a bracelet, he stood close until she could barely breathe.

"I'd love to get that for you, Rose. May I?"

Rose shook her head. "Just looking. Something I don't need, but thanks." Throat parched, she moved on, feeling light-headed as she made her way towards other stalls. The sun baked the back of her head.

Passing the market, they headed towards the crowded village, a light breeze fanning her face as she spotted a perfumery, more apartments above an array of cafes and restaurants, with passers-by squeezing between narrow spaces on the uneven ground. Archways and cobblestone streets led them uphill and Rose's feet started aching.

"Are you all right?"

She nodded as they faced a church and guests for what looked like a wedding. "You can't say that Italy doesn't have churches. It's the major attraction."

"Exactly, and a wedding's happening." Gianni stopped in his tracks with his hands on his hips, watching as people wearing evening attire climbed the few steps inside the church. Muffled voices echoed out. A loud bunch of teenagers teased each other until one of the friends got shoved into Gianni. The jolt pushed him nearer to Rose, their faces inches from one another.

Time stood still. Their eyes locked. Gianni's lips parted as he slowly drew a hand across her jaw, setting her heart racing. He flicked a strand of hair away from over her eye, as if not caring if others watched them. In the heat of the moment, her heart burned with desire and her hands sweated as he planted his lips on hers. He explored her mouth with tenderness.

"Ooh, how romantic," said a young female voice in the distance.

Rose blushed and she quickly broke the kiss and shifted back. The young woman gave her a cheeky grin before heading off with her loud group of friends.

She couldn't breathe and her surroundings appeared surreal when Gianni's touch drew her back to the present. "Let's keep going," she said.

Gianni stared. "Sorry."

Rose angled her head. "For what?"

Gianni clenched his hands as he stood against the wall of a seating area. "I shouldn't have kissed you. It was a mistake."

She didn't think so but lied. "You're right."

He averted her eyes. "You'll be leaving soon, anyway, so why complicate things? But..."

How could he say it like that?

CHAPTER 15

Rose lowered her head, her chin trembling. Her stomach clenched, and she felt the need to vomit. What was he saying? Was he only using her for fun and didn't care about her at all? It was as if he did this every day with women, but for her, it meant something. She couldn't imagine not seeing him again. Most likely he had other women in his pocket, just like her ex-boyfriend, Hugh. She wouldn't be making that same mistake, trusting a man she hardly knew. "But what?"

He shrugged. "Let's see the rest of Pienza, as we'll be leaving for Montalcino soon."

"Of course." She smiled reassuringly.

Spots flashed in her vision as she strolled alongside him with a painful tightness in her throat. She got the sense that Gianni was holding back about something, but what?

After getting back into the vehicle, Rose stared through the window of the limousine, aware of how close Gianni's thigh was to hers. His hands rested on his legs as he intermittently gazed in her direction. The citrus smell of his cologne made her yearn for his kiss again, but what was the point? She'd be leaving soon.

She felt the rough terrain beneath her as she fixated on rows upon rows of vineyards against the mountainous backdrop of Tuscany with its green and yellow hues and tiny billows of clouds in the brilliant blue sky. The vastness of the land had an energetic glow and the huddle of trees and plantations gave her peace amidst ruminations about the man before her.

Her phone buzzed in her bag. She answered the unknown number. "Hello."

"Hi Rose. It's Guido. How's your trip going?"

"Great, Guido. How are you?" She saw Gianni flinch beside her.

"Sorry to bother you, but we have a deadline on your decision about the villa. Any idea what you plan to do yet?"

She sighed, hating to disappoint the friendly man. "Sorry, Guido. I've decided not to sell the villa. It's too special to me."

"Okay then. Not a problem. But if you change your mind, we have a small window of time to change things."

"Okay, but I doubt it." After ending the call, she turned and noticed Gianni's pallor, his hands clenching by his sides. "Are you all right?"

He hesitated, avoiding her eyes. "You're not selling the villa?"

She shook her head. "No, it's too sentimental."

He still avoided her. "What are your plans for the villa, then?"

"Not sure yet, but I'm sure by the time I leave, I'll figure it out."

Gianni rubbed the back of his neck, shaking his leg and tapping his foot on the floor. "Listen, I need to tell you something. I..."

Rose tilted her head, curling a brow. "What is it?"

"I... I... Oh, shit. This is going to sound crazy, but I didn't mean to... Oh, Christ."

Rose swallowed, wondering if he wanted to confess to being a serial killer or a pauper, and waited as he kept rubbing his neck. "Just tell me, Gianni. It can't be that bad."

Breathing heavily, he said, "I'm the property developer in charge of selling your villa. It was my dad's wish to tear it down for his friend who wants to gift the apartments to his children. I was planning to get it all organised because not only do I help out with the winery, but I own a property development company too."

Rose's heart constricted, with a dry, coppery taste to her mouth. *What the hell?* She hadn't heard right, had she? "Are you serious?" She scoffed. "You lied to me."

Gianni grabbed her hand, but she snatched it away and shifted in her seat as if she couldn't get far enough away. He stiffened, his hand still in the air as if wanting to reach her. She rested back against her seat, staring through the window but not seeing anything but starbursts behind her eyelids, taking her back to when Hugh had lied to her. It was happening again. She sure could pick them.

"Please let me explain."

Rose clenched her hands, her breathing erratic. The driver turned as if he wanted to say something, but then faced the front again. "What's there to explain? You lied, plain and simple."

"I didn't want our friendship to affect your decision, so my friend Sergio spoke on my behalf to be objective in the potential sale. I like you, Rose, and I didn't want to pressure you into selling, but at the same time—"

"You wanted me to sell? Is that why we're going out now? So you could convince me to sell? Are you just using me for the villa?"

He flinched. "Are you kidding? Of course not. I hated lying to you. I was planning to tell you the truth today, but we were having such a great time and I didn't want to ruin it. I knew you'd be mad about this." He toyed with his nails. "I wanted to spend a special day with you. I am sorry for not telling you the truth, but I needed someone who was level-headed. Sergio was happy to take my place."

"I just can't believe this. I trusted you."

"We wanted you to have a fair proposal without me being involved after we'd met in Montepulciano. I liked you from the start, Rose. I didn't want to get to know you from a business transaction. You even mentioned how property developers act like sharks, and I didn't want you to see me that way. I am sorry."

"Oh, so now this is my fault you didn't tell me?" He shook his head, then looked away. She couldn't think straight while she hated him with a passion. He was a fraud, not knowing who he truly was. Where was the trust now? "I want you to take me home. I refuse to go anywhere else with you, Gianni. I can no longer trust you."

A gentle hand on her shoulder made her melt as intense feelings made her brain turn to mush. She savoured the gentleness of his touch, his leg brushing against hers, and his lips close to her ear as she kept peering through the window. His shallow breathing and warm caress against her shoulder trailing down her arm made her think he was genuinely sorry. But she had got caught in Hugh's lies because of her irrational feelings and she couldn't do that again. "Please, Rose. I need you to understand why I did it. Not for anything malicious, but because I cared. I wanted to get to know you as me and not as the man who was trying to get you to sell your villa. If you don't want to sell, then I'll deal with my dad. But you need to know he's dying, and I wanted to grant him his wish before he leaves us."

Her face shifted in his direction, gasping. "What?"

"He has an aggressive cancer. The doctors said he might only have a few more months, so I wasn't thinking straight. I wanted his approval...to make him happy one last time before he dies. I know it's no excuse, but you need to realise what I was thinking at the time. It was important for him to help out his friend, but if you can't, then I'll find another piece of land for Alfonzo. No problem."

Her hands carved through her hair, her posture slightly slumping. She didn't want to go through this again. A father dying.

Gianni was going through his own pain, and getting too attached to him was a bad idea. "I am sorry about your dad. I...I struggled when my dad passed. But don't think I forgive you, Gianni. You were dishonest and that's not okay." She felt a tear stream down her cheek and Gianni wiped it away as he came closer to her.

He inched forward. "I know, and I am so sorry."

"I don't like what you did but putting it in perspective when someone's dying makes it all appear trivial. Still, it's wrong."

He nodded. "It sucks that death is the surest thing in life. You were young when your father died. At least I've had more time with my dad. But it still hurts." He cleared his throat. "How did you and your mother manage on your own without him?"

She shrugged. "One day at a time." Despite still being mad at Gianni for lying to her, in the bigger scheme of things, it was nothing compared to the deaths of their loved ones. The pain Gianni must be going through, she wouldn't impose on her worst enemy. Maybe she understood wanting to give his father peace before he died. If he cared about her, perhaps it would have been hard for him to have a businesslike approach in their relationship when they'd started out as friends. Could she forgive him?

The silence in the car for the rest of the trip gave her the time to process everything until the driver spoke up. Could she learn to forgive him when he was going through a traumatic time with his father? She wasn't so sure because he had broken her trust, and trust didn't come easily to her. "Are we taking Rose home, Mr. Abbate?"

Gianni raised a brow as she glanced in his direction. "Rose?"

She didn't trust him but wanted to believe he had a kind, soft heart. "Let's keep to the schedule for now. But don't for a minute think I've forgiven you."

The light in his eyes just increased her feelings towards him tenfold. "Understood."

CHAPTER 16

Rose leaned back in the stainless-steel chair with her elbows resting on an ash-black round table set over brick-tiled flooring underneath a pergola. A steel fence separated her and Gianni from the mountainous terrain below, with a creeper along the roof, brush over hilly ground, and shades of beige and green hills. A picnic basket covered with a red, chequered cloth hung out, filled with bags of bread and Pecorino cheese. Nutty smells of the cheese, freshly made Ciabatta bread, and assorted jams filled the air as she watched Gianni spread pear jam over a slice, spilling pieces of it on the table. He passed her the knife after his face had reddened, as if from embarrassment.

"No thanks. I'll use the other knife and cut this cheese. It smells amazing." She cut a piece and plonked it on a slice of bread. Tasting it was like heaven, with pungent tones of mild spices and seared butter. It was hard and crumbly in texture, and had a strong, salty flavour. She relished the softness and heat of the bread, which had satisfied her hunger.

Gianni cut up more cheese on the chopping board and added more jam onto the bread and a piece of another type of Pecorino cheese. "You need to try this jam. It goes well with the cheese."

She nodded. "Okay, fine." With a smear of jam on the bread and a slice of cheese on top, Rose took a bite. "Yes, it goes well with the jam. It's even tastier."

He smirked. "I told you."

Rose devoured the last remnants of bread, then took a sip of coke which quenched her thirst in the scorching heat. Her body sweated, and the humidity of the Tuscan heat made it feel as if she hadn't washed her hair that day. "What an amazing view."

"Hmm, I agree," he said as he stared at her with one hand resting under his jaw.

She blushed, assuming he was talking about her. "Don't think you're getting off lightly, Gianni. I might understand why you lied to me, but it doesn't mean I'm happy about it."

"I know, and I'm glad you understand how worried I am about my dad right now. It's why I'm helping him out at the vineyard. I'm taking his place."

She wondered what would happen once he died. "What was it like for you growing up in Tuscany?"

Gianni's eyes peered into the distance. "Good and bad." He frowned. "Growing up, my parents were always busy with the business. I helped out a bit as I got older, but they hardly ever did anything fun with me. I don't have siblings, so I was alone most of the time. I had babysitters, mainly cousins, but I always wished we could go to the beach or watch a soccer game. I always felt the business was more important than I was. If I went missing, I doubt they would've noticed."

Rose's heart went out to him. "I'm sorry, Gianni, but I'm sure they would have noticed. They wanted to build a future for you—and look at you now. Do you have any nice memories of your family?"

He gazed in the distance. "I remember one time my dad took me fishing, and we caught the biggest fish you could imagine. He told me stories of his childhood and we laughed and hugged. It was the first time I'd seen him relax, and I wanted more of those times. It's the only one I remember of us doing something other than working together."

"How old were you?"

"Eleven. I know he tried to organise other events, but something always came up with the vineyards. One problem or another. But you know what hurts the most, Rose?" She shook her head. "When I started the business after I did my business degree and property development training, he said 'If it wasn't for the family name, you wouldn't have succeeded in property development. It's because of the strong Abbate name and backing.' It was such a slap in the face, and since then, I could never get my father's approval for anything I did." His chin lowered to his chest, and he stared down at his hands.

Rose squeezed his shoulder. "That must have been hard to hear, but I can tell you work your butt off, Gianni. You need to believe in yourself. He obviously has high expectations, and I assume you've succeeded in your business." She couldn't imagine what he was going through, her heart burning at his pain. Was that why this villa arrangement was important to him? Did he need to prove he could succeed in property development with this deal for his father's friend? Should she reconsider selling the villa?

He gave her a reassuring smile. "It's fine. My business does well, and he knows it. He's not the type to express how he feels. I'm the opposite. I tend to over share." She wanted to tell him he hadn't done that after lying to her, but she remained tight-lipped. Surely, she understood why he did it. "I am sorry about your father."

Rose put another piece of cheese into her mouth, then washed it down with her drink. "When we found out my dad was sick, my mum and I cared for him. It hurt like hell when he died. Like this great, big, gaping hole appeared in the middle of my chest. I couldn't breathe. I couldn't sleep, and I couldn't eat. It was much worse for my mum. It felt like something in my life was missing, and yet...."

Gianni shifted closer in his chair. "And yet?"

"My dad was too nice to people. They usually stepped all over him. He always looked for the good in people, but for some, it doesn't exist. One time, he started a cabinet-making business with his friend, who did more of the accounts work. After about three years into the business, the bastard friend took all the profits they kept in their shared account and skipped the country. My dad lost his share of the money he'd saved in those three years. And before that, this same friend had stolen one of my dad's motorbikes and sold it online at a hugely marked-up price to make money."

"You're kidding," said Gianni.

"I kid you not. But my dad forgave him after his friend handed him the money he got from the bike. I got the feeling that he didn't give my dad everything. I told him not to trust the guy. I was only a teenager, but I sensed something fishy about him. But my dad said that people deserve a second chance. Then look what happened." She ached inside, thinking about her father's pain. "Once he got caught in a business scam from this wealthy guy who wanted to get richer. I've heard a few horror stories about millionaires, and I vowed to let no one step on me. I work damn hard to reach my goals."

Gianni coughed. "It sounds like your dad was amazing. I wish I could have got to know him."

"He was, but too trusting. The poor man suffered with his disease, his fake friends, and his own battered childhood. He didn't deserve any of that, Gianni. None of it."

"I know. He didn't." He moved his chair next to hers and put an arm around her shoulder. She edged in closer to him and fought back tears. The touch of his warm hand against her skin calmed her and she felt safe in his arms.

"I loved him with all my heart, Gianni. I'm so grateful I got twenty amazing years with him, and I know he's still with me." She pointed to her heart. "In here is what counts."

Gianni stroked her cheek. "I am sorry, Rose. I wish I could make the pain go away."

She could no longer hold in the hurt and loss, and felt tears sting her cheeks as Gianni wrapped her in his arms. She savoured the comfort of his touch.

CHAPTER 17

G ianni stood outside Abbate Wines with a young couple and their rambunctious son who kicked loose stones on the ground. The sun warmed his scalp, and the light breeze brushed his cheeks. "We have a jumping castle out back for your son and refreshments inside. How old is he?"

The woman, Mary, came from England and wore a tight-fitting floral dress with her hair tied up in a loose bun. "He's five, but going on fifteen. The jumping castle would keep him busy. Do you distribute your wine to shops, Mr. Abbate?"

Before he replied, his breath stopped when he spotted Rose climbing the steps with Luna. For a moment, he was speechless because of the way her sundress wrapped tightly around her waist, her long legs seeming to go on forever, and the outline of her smooth, tanned neck. She looked beautiful, as always. "We sell direct to our buyers. It's about providing a personal touch and direct communication. But we are looking at possibly distributing in Montepulciano stores in the near future."

Gianni recalled their day out a few days ago and hadn't been able to get her out of his head. He had wanted to see her again, so he'd invited her to this family fun day at the winery. It was a way to build the business, and an event his father had run twice a year. If they did these more often, it'd give them more exposure among tourists and locals. He could even contribute financially to the vineyard.

His heart broke when Rose had cried over her father. The only thing he could do was wrap her in his arms and make her feel safe. Luckily, she forgave him for hiding his true identity, but how would he explain to his father that she didn't want to sell?

Gianni nodded to Rose, and she waved, then grabbed a drink from a waiter circling the winery. He turned back to the woman. "We also have animals and a clown show, which I'm sure your son will love."

She grinned. "Thank you," said the woman. She made her way towards her son, who waved his hands and attempted to grab Rose's wine, but by the time Gianni reached her, the wine had spilled over her dress.

Gianni touched her shoulder. "You'll need to wash that off."

Mary yanked on her son's arm. "Come here, now." The boy sulked but soon recovered, facing Rose and watching her stare at Gianni.

"Ooh, ooh, you love him," said the boy, grinning.

Redness lined Rose's throat as she stared at the ground while Gianni cleared his throat, heat warming his face.

Mary shook her head. "I am so sorry," she said to Rose. "He gets excited during these gatherings. My apologies."

"Not a problem. It'll easily come out," Rose said.

When the couple and their son moved away, Gianni smiled. "He liked you, but come with me, Rose. I'll help you get that out. It's going to smell."

"Thanks." She turned to Luna. "I'll be back soon."

Luna gave her a cheeky grin. "Take your time, girl. I'll go around back and check out the animals. I might even enjoy the clown show." She winked and walked off.

Gianni laughed. "She's fun, isn't she?"

"She is a riot."

He beamed.

Rose followed him inside, pushing through crowds of people holding wine glasses and chattering loudly. Others tasted wines and purchased bottles.

He took her through to the staff area and headed to the sink. From underneath it, he pulled out a washcloth. "Here, use this."

She took it from him, and their hands touched. Swallowing hard, she ran it underneath the tap, and wiped below her chest as she bent down slowly. He couldn't help gazing at the centre of her chest and the outline of her bra, wondering what it would feel like to taste her there. What would it feel like to brush his hands over her nipples and trace the outline of her breasts? *Stop!*

After rinsing the cloth, she placed it into the sink. "This is a great turn-out."

He nodded. "It does well for business. Even the adults enjoy these family fun days. Come. Let's go around the back."

They walked on the grassy uneven ground until they reached an enclosure with a group of cows standing on piles of scattered hay. Small children and their parents patted the animals through the gaps in the wooden fence. One of the staff members, Bruno, an elderly, easy-going man, waved his hands in the air as he leaned in towards the children and talked about milk production and cheese-making.

On one side was a table of snacks and drinks where Luna stood, biting into a piece of cheese on a cracker. "You should try this cheese, Rose. It's the best."

Rose and Gianni approached, picking at the assorted cheeses and adding them to their plastic plates, in addition to a variety of cold cuts: salami, prosciutto, ham, and home-made sausage.

"This smells and looks amazing," said Rose.

Bruno approached Gianni. "The clown has a few questions before he starts the show. Would you mind going inside? I told the kids they can come with me."

Gianni swallowed, not wanting to leave Rose, who smelled of fresh flowers. But what choice did he have? "Sure." He turned to Rose and Luna. "Excuse me, ladies. I'll be back soon." He walked off with Bruno and the group of children, with their parents following behind. When he looked over his shoulder, he found Rose staring at him as if she would miss him. Did she care about him as much as he did about her?

"Okay, what the hell is going on with you guys? You keep staring at each other as if you want to have sex right here," said Luna.

Rose's face warmed as she tuned out the sounds of cows mooing and crowds talking around them. The Tuscan panorama was tranquil despite the muffled voices of visitors and the screaming, excited children who ran behind Gianni and the man who worked for him. She savoured the greenery and billowing clouds in the blue sky, and the clumps of trees and sloping mountains. Smells of smoke, dust, dirt, and cypress trees filled the air around her as she sweated at the back of her neck in the hard-hitting sun and humid wind. "Well...."

"Well what, girl?"

"We...aah, sort of kissed."

Luna's eyes dilated. "Wow. Oh, wow. How was it, and what is happening with you guys? Are you going out, having sex, or what? And why didn't you tell me, girl?"

Rose laughed and put up a hand, her light sandals sinking into a wet patch of grass. She moved to a dry patch. "That's a lot of questions, but no, we are not having sex, and he stopped the kiss, realising it wasn't right. I believe him."

Luna threw a cracker into her mouth, chewing and talking with her mouth full. "What do you mean, it's not right? You're a woman, he's a man. Do the math?"

Rose loved Luna and remembered having fun times with her at school. She had changed a little. "I don't live here, for one. Two, I can't see a future for us when neither of us plans to move. And three, I don't need another relationship in which I can't trust a guy who keeps secrets."

Luna lifted a brow, so she explained how he had lied to her about being a property developer.

"Oh, come on, Rose. He didn't know you like he does now. He probably thought you'd judge him and didn't want you to think he could influence your decision to sell the villa. The main thing is that he eventually told you the truth."

"Maybe, but it won't work. Long distance doesn't work; he said it himself. Besides, I don't even think he's looking for a relationship, and neither am I. I don't know if he feels what I do about him. If we keep our distance, it'll make it easier when I finally leave. I can't get too attached. He's got too much going on in his life right now."

"You're kidding yourself. I can see the steam between you guys. At least enjoy yourself with him. No harm in that. You can have delicious sex with him for the next six weeks, at least. What great memories you'll make, girl."

Could Rose risk her heart and take a chance on a man she couldn't stop thinking about? He was on her mind during the day and in her dreams. It was impossible to sleep when he kept torturing her inside her head. But why go through the pain again?

CHAPTER 18

The next day, Gianni rubbed the back of his neck and sighed. "Keep your voice down, Dad. Please."

"I had to hear it from Guido, didn't I? Why the hell won't Rose sell?" His father was in his robe inside his bedroom, pacing and clenching his hands so tight that Gianni could see the white in his knuckles.

Gianni calmed his breathing, placing a hand on his father's shoulder, but he shoved it away. "Please, Dad. She wants to change it into some kind of writer's retreat. It's admirable because she wants to help the community."

His father glared. "Community? What community? It's not the Italians, it's writers. Who cares about them? This is about making a promise to me and getting that woman to sell, no matter what. We need the damn land."

Gianni's chest constricted as he turned away from his father and stared out the window, wishing he didn't have a father who never believed in him; wishing he didn't have a father who put him down at every opportunity. Why did his father make him feel like that ten-year-old boy, starved for affection when he wanted to be taken to a sports game or a movie, or even out for an ice cream? Why could he never be good enough for this man? Why couldn't he be accepted as he was, unconditionally? "Please calm down. The doctors said you need to limit your stress. It's why I didn't tell you. Because I want you to save your energy. I'll find another brilliant piece of land for Alfonzo. Believe in me, please, Father."

He pulled the blankets over and sat back in bed with his back against the headrest, glaring at his son. "No, we wanted that land. Your job is to sweeten Rose, wine and dine her, do anything to change her mind. Hell, marry the woman just to get her on side. I don't bloody well care what you do. Just do it." His eyes hardened. "We still have time before she plans to leave. You mentioned she's working here for over a month?"

He nodded. "Yes." He pursed his lips, his breathing shallow, as he grabbed the edge of his father's blanket, squeezing it tight as if wringing out his frustrations. How the hell could his father ask him to use Rose like that? It was not his style, and he wasn't about to start now. "I am doing no such thing. She deserves better than that and has made her decision."

His father pointed a finger. "No, you listen to me. If you're already seeing her as a friend, then talk to her about the benefits of selling. No harm in talking about the villa, is there? She can take time off work or go on a holiday with the money she'll make. Hell, you can even up the price."

Gianni threw the edge of the blanket, glaring. "No, you listen to me. It's bad enough you put me down at every chance you get, but you will not disrespect Rose. She deserves to keep her childhood memories in that home, and you have no right to ruin it for her."

His father tilted his head, pressing a finger across his chin. "If I was a betting man, I'd say you care about this woman."

Gianni leaned forward, inches from his father's face. "Her name is Rose, not 'this woman,' and I like Rose. She's a friend, and I won't have you treating her like rubbish. She's a human being and deserves the world." Before his father could reply, he stormed out and slammed the bedroom door. He kicked at a pair of slippers and walked outside, grateful to breathe in the fresh air, even if it was sultry. Pushing back his guilt, he wished he had handled his father differently, especially when the man was dying. But he wouldn't listen to reason.

Rose hovered over her student, Julie, the sun casting a shadow through the bare window. "You're doing great work." She grabbed the notebook and read a scene from a suspense novel. "I love the foreshadowing here. Now you can add in the twists and create those red herrings."

Julie beamed. "I'll work on that tonight." She exhaled. "You've been great with the class, Rose. I wish I could keep you in my pocket when I return to England."

Rose handed back her notebook. "We can exchange email addresses, so feel free to send me questions you have or any drafts I can pore over. Happy to do that."

Julie rose and piled her belongings into a satchel. "That would be great. Thank you so much." She picked up her bag. "Oh, and about that writer's retreat you're thinking about—count me in as your first customer when it's ready. Such a great way to offer ongoing help, particularly for those struggling to write for a living."

"If I can do it, Julie, anyone can. It takes discipline and persistence. I'm happy to see that many people can do it full-time and make a living. But it's only an idea for now. I don't know if I can pull it off."

"I know you can." Julie wrapped her arms around her. "I'll see you tomorrow." The woman walked out of the room with a spring in her step.

Rose walked to her table and closed her resource books, gathered up loose papers and pens, and inserted them into her bag when her phone rang with a face-time call. Gina and Dalia were on the other end. "Hi, girls. I've missed you so much. How are you both?"

Dalia grinned. "Great, Rose. Luca and I are taking a trip to Bali in a week, so I can't wait to have a break from work."

"Sounds amazing. Have a great time if I don't speak to you." If only Rose could have a love like that.

Gina displayed herself on the screen. "What's new with the villa?"

Rose sat in her seat and leaned back, taking a breath. "I've decided not to sell. I'm thinking of using it as a writer's guest house or retreat to help struggling writers. What do you think?"

Gina squinted. "Is that profitable? Don't you think it'll be hard to run it while you're back here? It is a pipe-dream, Rose." She wouldn't expect anything less than worry and realism from her friend.

Dalia pushed her aside. "Do not listen to her, Rose. It's a great idea and one which would reap rewards, whether it's profitable or not. I'd definitely use it if I was a writer."

"Thanks, Dals. It's only a thought at this stage, but Gina might be right. I don't know how it would work if I'm in Melbourne."

"You could get someone to manage it for you," said Dalia. "Oh, and how's Mr. Handsome? Gianni, isn't it?"

Rose blushed, and the fluttering in her heart intensified. Why couldn't she get the man out of her mind? All she thought about were those lips on hers, skin on skin, and his powerful arms around her waist? Oh, she missed him like she'd never missed a man before. He was a pipe-dream too. "We're friends, nothing more."

"But you'd like it to be more, wouldn't you, Rose?" Dalia put up a hand towards Gina as if daring her to speak.

She nodded. "Yes. I've never felt this close to any guy before."

Gina spoke from behind Dalia. "Do not get attached. If you do, you'll get hurt when you leave. He sounds too good to be true, anyway. I wouldn't trust a good-looking Italian man who'll most likely use you, knowing you'll be leaving soon."

Rose's chest ached. What if he hurt her like her ex? What if she got attached, but it was too late? Would there really be no harm in enjoying each other while they could?

"Listen, Rose. You should keep it simple and see where it leads. If you let fear stop you, you'll regret it when you come back. If I listened to my critical voice, I'd never be in a relationship with Luca. We love each other more every day. Do not miss out on any opportunities you have. If he's genuine, then go for it."

"You think so?" said Rose.

"I know so," said Dalia.

"Be careful," said Gina. "I don't want you getting hurt."

"Oh, but I still have over a month here and I might consider..." She stopped in her tracks when Gianni walked inside, grinning. How much had he heard? "Listen, ladies. I have to go, but I'll be in touch soon." She ended the call and faced the man whose muscles were accented by tight-fitting black shorts and a skin-tight white polo t-shirt. He bit his upper lip as if he was nervous. Rose swallowed and got lost in his eyes as he remained fixed to the spot.

CHAPTER 19

Rose wondered how much of her conversation Gianni had heard. A redness across her cheeks made her bow down. "This is a surprise. What are you doing here?"

Gianni pinched the skin at his throat and bounced his foot on the floor. He paced across to the window, drawing away the curtain and peering through. "I wanted to see what you were up to after your work here."

Rose yearned to have his arms around her, but she remained in place. "I planned to go shopping in the centre for retail therapy. But I can do that another day. No problem if you have something else in mind."

His eyes lit up with hope. "Can I come with you?"

Rose's heart warmed. "I would like that." She picked up her satchel. "I am ready when you are." She pushed forward, carrying her satchel, and followed him outside.

Stepping onto the uneven cobblestones, her eyes flickered to his tanned, muscled legs while his shorts hugged him tightly around the waist. The t-shirt enhanced his flat, taut stomach and broad shoulders.

The quiet walk to the centre of Montepulciano was awkward, as if they were both processing what had happened between them. She couldn't get that kiss out of her head.

The gentle way he moaned, and the way his skin felt against her body... But in all fairness, where could their relationship go if not towards a sad end?

Walking alongside Gianni down the sloping street made her heart soar as his shoulder brushed against hers. They passed by a women's clothing store, souvenir shop, wine cellar, real estate shopfront, a sweet store, and an ice cream shop until they came to the clothing store where Rose wanted to try on a summer dress.

She took the step up inside the store that had an orange summer dress hanging on a mannequin. It had thin straps and the skirt was long and flowing. "I like this one."

Gianni prodded her further into the store. "Try it on."

"I'll browse first." She cleared her throat and Gianni walked behind her, glancing through the clothing racks when a saleswoman with stunning features and bright eyes approached. "Just looking for now." The woman smiled but continued to stand close by, her eyes darting to Gianni with interest. Her stomach tightened. The man could have his pick of women.

Rose swiped through blouses and picked a floral one she liked, then moved over to more dresses when Gianni held up a bright crimson dress that featured a low neckline and a high split on the side. "No thanks. It's a bit too revealing for my taste."

Gianni gave her a cheeky grin. "Hmm. I don't mind. Let me buy this for you."

She shook her head. "No, thanks. I have my own money. You don't need to get me anything, but I appreciate the thought." She found the orange dress and a beige one with a halter neck to try on.

Several other women and men walked inside while Gianni stood close to the fitting room as she tried on the orange dress. Coming out of the room, she stood in front of a long mirror while Gianni devoured her with his eyes, as if he wanted to eat her. It was sexy.

"What do you think?"

His eyes lit up as he licked his lips. "Beautiful," said Gianni as he eyed her from top to bottom like he could imagine what was underneath. Tingles ran over her body.

She headed back inside the fitting room, pulled off the orange dress, and replaced it with the beige one, pressing down on it until she stepped out of the cubicle. She fought against the heat in her cheeks as she fanned herself. *Hell*. The way his eyes devoured her as if he could see underneath her clothes...

Finally heading back out, she stood in front of the mirror. "I like this one too." Gianni nodded, beaming.

She picked up all the clothes in the dressing room and sorted the items she wanted to buy, then handed them to the saleswoman. "I won't take the blouse, only the dresses."

"Of course," the woman said as she entered the items on the cash register while gazing at Gianni, who quickly handed her his credit card. The woman accepted the card.

"No, no, I'll pay." She faced him. "Please, this was my idea. I can pay."

He waved her hand away, shaking his head. "Please, my treat. A going-away gift."

Two women stood behind her. She didn't want to make a fuss and hold up the line, so she sighed. "Fine. Thank you."

Rose wondered why he felt the need to buy her a dress, fighting against guilt that she let him pay. Not that he would budge on that. But after this trip, she'd no longer see him. She could only savour her precious days with a man who might have stolen her heart.

They ambled back outside onto the uneven surface, with crowds walking uphill while they walked downhill past a bag shop. Gianni backtracked and headed inside the store. The apartments with balconies on either side kept the street contained and the mumbling voices surrounding them kept the city alive. A few compact cars were parked on the side of the street where people had to squeeze through to access the path.

"Why are we here? Do you need a bag?"

He shook his head. "Tell me which one you like, Rose. You need a new bag."

Rose angled her head, her racing heart making her dizzy. "I don't need this, Gianni. I can't let you keep paying for me when I'm my own woman. I have my own money. Let's keep moving." She ogled a tan bag with a short strap and clasp then put it down, gasping at the price tag.

"Do you like that one?"

She grimaced. "No, please. You already bought me two dresses, so that's it." As she walked outside the store, she expected him to follow, but he was retrieving a plastic bag with the tan bag inside of it.

Gianni stepped outside and pushed the bag into her hand. "It's yours because I know you like it. I noticed you recoil at the price tag, Rose. I don't mind. Consider it a gift from a special friend who is saying sorry. I added a wallet in there too because I noticed your current one is old."

Rose's face flushed again, thinking he was attempting to make up for their argument and the way he had hurt her. Guilt money. She struggled to find the right words and pinched the bottom of her lip as she remained rooted to the spot outside the shop, people passing her by and gazing at the two of them. "Why did you do that, Gianni?"

They resumed their walk, spotting Carabinieri as they made their way towards the Piazza Grande. They sat on the steps while the sun warmed her scalp.

"I care about you, Rose, and want to give you as many gifts as I can. These are things you need, so please accept them."

"I know you have your vineyard and your property development work, but the way you easily buy things tells me you don't worry about money."

Gianni gazed at the church and passers-by. "I do okay."

He did more than okay, she thought. "How about I get you something?" Rose asked.

He chuckled. "An Aperol Spritz will do me. Perhaps lunch too."

CHAPTER 20

Three days later, Gianni climbed the stairs and approached the room where Rose was teaching when he stopped in his tracks. She was a vision as he watched her bow her head, eyes closed as if she was meditating. Her breathing appeared shallow and her hands clasped and rested on the table.

He hated spying on her, but his heart raced as if his chest might explode, and his throat became parched. Even his hands dampened at the idea that she might reject him. They were only seeing each other as friends, he reminded himself.

Gianni stepped forward and took a calming breath as Rose jumped in fright. She abruptly closed her laptop with shaky hands and looked at him square in the face, biting her bottom lip as she threaded a hand through her hair.

All he wanted to do was pull her out of her chair and hold her tight, glide his hands down her body and taste every inch of her. He wanted to nibble the side of her neck and bury his tongue deep inside her mouth, making her climax with deep and lustful kisses. Gianni wanted her in his bed to savour her like he'd never savoured a woman before. He wanted to make her scream his name. He wanted her to think only of him when they made love.

The clicking of her low heels alerted him to the present. "Sorry. I didn't mean to scare you. Are you all right?"

Rose gripped her laptop, putting it inside her satchel, and stood before him. She was wearing a flimsy off the shoulder white blouse that showed the outline of smooth, tanned skin across her upper arms, tempting him to trace his hands over them. Her loose-fitting black skirt fell down to her ankles, and he was curious about what was underneath. "I'm fine. I was decompressing from the energy of the class."

"You? I thought you loved that high energy."

She nodded. "I do, but I haven't been sleeping much lately, and today, the class tired me out. But I love the energy too."

"Understandable. I admire anyone who can teach. I wouldn't have that in me." Her eyes glistened while he fidgeted, feeling as if the heat had ramped up. "Listen. I thought we might have dinner together. I'd like to cook for you at my place."

"You cook?" He nodded. Touching the centre of her chest, she rubbed as if nervous and curled a brow. "Sounds good."

"Great. You can follow me in your rental car." She picked up her satchel then he made his way down the stairs as she followed behind, the smell of her flowery perfume making him want her even more.

The tree-lined path outside the building left shadows on the ground as Rose caught up to him. They were passing by a giant blue teacup on the gravel path as he walked through dirt and debris when Rose knocked her shoulder into a tree trunk, wincing. He pulled her towards him. "Are you okay?"

She blushed and rubbed her upper arm. "Must have been distracted. All good." Tilting her head, she took in a gulp of air. Inching her way forward, her eyes turned upward as he yearned to flick a hair strand away from her eyes, but he didn't. "Let's go."

As they stood transfixed opposite each other, his heart ached for her; he couldn't wait to get her alone. The way she gazed as if seeing into his soul touched him and he couldn't imagine a time when he didn't know her. How could she have been missing from his life all these years?

Rose broke their moment and made her way down the path towards the car park. The silence was broken by the sound of drums from opposite them, where a group of young children and people dressed in medieval clothing were marching around the village with crowds following. They stomped up and down the streets.

"What is that?"

"Oh, that's the history of the village they demonstrate through re-enactments and performances of medieval history. It gives the tourists something else to do. It's a way of honouring the history of this beautiful Tuscan town."

Approaching his car, he waited for Rose to step inside her own so she could follow him to his house, attempting to take his mind off every intimate thing he wanted to do to her. Would she welcome it? No harm in fun.

Gianni gripped the knife and chopped an onion on a board while Rose stood alongside him and cut up garlic. "Do you want to know the secret of an Italian sauce?"

Rose jokingly pushed into him with her shoulder, smirking. "Oh, come on, Gianni. I have an Italian background. I know the answer to that."

He put down his knife, his eyes fixated on hers. "What is it?"

"It's basil, parsley, garlic, and rosemary?"

He turned to his onion then wiped his hands on his apron. "Very good, but you forgot one thing." She angled her head. "Organic fresh tomatoes. I just picked them off the vine earlier. Care to grab them?"

She piled the basil onto a plate and grinned. "You grow your own tomatoes?"

"Of course I do. I grow herbs and a few other vegetables, but I have a gardener managing it all. Who has the time?"

Rose swung open the fridge and pulled out a bowl of tomatoes. "I'll put these in a pot to boil them." She turned to him. "Where are your pots?" He pointed and Rose picked one up, bending down to reach the bottom. His eyes flicked over to her smooth, feminine thighs as her skirt lifted. He quickly turned back to his onion and threw the pieces into a bowl. Walking back to the fridge, Gianni picked up the plate of minced meat and handed it to Rose, who had turned on the stove. "I can season the meat." Her hands glided off his as she dropped it on the bench.

Gianni handed her an egg, salt, pepper, and parmesan cheese. "If you'd like to add anything else it's fine."

She cracked the egg into the meat. "Yes, a touch of thyme if you have it." He walked over to his pantry and retrieved a jar. "Here you go." When she started mixing all the ingredients into the meat with a fork, Gianni stopped her. "No, you need to be Italian and use your hands."

Rose shook her head. "Oh no, the meat's too cold. I hate cooking that way."

He laughed. "What kind of Italian are you, not using your greatest tools?" Standing behind her with his body pressed against hers, he manoeuvred his arms underneath hers. clasping her hands, and together, they mixed in the herbs and egg into the meat, creating a messy mixture.

The way her body felt with her bottom pressing hard against his crotch and her bare shoulder against his own sent shivers down his spine. Rose's breathing seemed to slow down as they worked the meat in silence. She leaned back against him, and he welcomed it and felt himself harden. The lavender smell of her hair as she shifted closer to him aroused him. They couldn't stay like this forever, so he pulled his hands away and washed them. *Get it together, man.*

Rose stood awkwardly at the counter, staring into the bowl until he finished at the tap. She walked to the sink and washed her own hands. "Excuse me. I need to go to the bathroom."

His vocal cords failed to work, but he nodded.

What the hell was going on with him? The action of mixing the meat with their hands joining together had been erotic and surreal, like nothing he'd ever experienced before. It was like he couldn't imagine living without her. He couldn't breathe, couldn't think, and couldn't sleep with her on his mind every single minute of every day.

He didn't want her to go back to Melbourne, such a long way away. He didn't want to stop seeing her after she had enriched his life ten-fold. He didn't want to feel this pressure from his father to make her change her mind about the villa. But what would he do once she left? Would he have this deep, empty space in his stomach?

The unthinkable ran through his mind. Maybe he was falling in love with a woman he could never have. But wasn't it better to enjoy the time she had left here rather than regret not getting the joy they could both experience? Life was too short.

Gianni headed over to the stove and forked a soft tomato, then switched off the gas. He emptied the pot of tomatoes into a colander inside the sink, placed them into a bowl and peeled them. Grabbing one tomato, he winced at the scorching heat of the fruit, as he pulled off the skin and threw it into a smaller bowl. By the time he'd finished, Rose still hadn't returned, and he wondered what had happened. Dead silence.

He rolled meat around his hands, shaped it into a ball, then dropped it onto a plate. By the time he reached his third meatball, footsteps sounded. He turned with a reassuring smile. "You okay?"

She nodded. "All good." Rose joined him in making meatballs, rolling each one around her palm as they worked in silence, the tension thick.

Say something, man. Gianni's breath hitched. "It's obvious you like cooking as much as I do. Who taught you to cook? Was it your mother?"

"My mother and great aunt. I remember one time, my aunt Maria showed me how to cook Crostoli. Instead of adding the self-raising flour, I added two cups of sugar and made a well in the centre, adding eggs, vanilla and lemon. I wondered why it wasn't thickening up and became more like shortbread."

He chuckled. "How could you mistake the flour for the sugar? What was your aunt doing at the time?"

"The packet of the sugar and flour looked basically the same, and obviously I didn't read the label properly. I was only eight, so give me a break." Rose took a breath. "She had taken a call and was busy on the phone, trusting me to add the ingredients after she'd only told me once. A young girl's attention span is short."

"What happened to your concoction?"

Rose finished rolling the last meatball into her hand and lay it on the plate. "We made shortbread instead, and it was delicious despite being too sweet. Who knows how many calories I added to my body?"

"All wasn't totally lost then."

Rose shook her head and washed her hands at the tap. Gianni stood behind her, his body pressed against her back. He ignored his desire when she faced him again. As he washed his hands, she sighed. "I really miss those times. Maria was always teaching me things." Her body stilled. "I could have used her wise counsel even now."

He angled his head, then grabbed the same pot and added parsley, garlic, onion, and rosemary to the hot oil, stirring it with a wooden spoon. "Why would you need her wise counsel now?" Was it about him?

She shrugged and retrieved the plate of meatballs, then dropped them gently into the oil. "You know. Just stuff. Life. Nothing major."

Was he not a major topic of discussion? Did she feel about him exactly how he felt about her? The signals were there, and he wanted to test the waters.

"Our teachings will only stop once we're six feet under. Life sucks sometimes."

Rose arched a brow. "How eloquent, Gianni. Should we add the tomatoes now?" He nodded, so she carried the bowl to the stove and gently poured in the tomatoes, tiny splashes spattering on to her blouse. "Oh, damn. Now my top's dirty."

"You can wash it off in the bathroom. I'll watch the sauce and get the spaghetti ready. I'll have a nice glass of wine ready for you too."

"Thanks." She walked off, and he found he could catch his breath again.

CHAPTER 21

R ose chewed the spaghetti, speaking in between bites as Gianni sipped his glass of wine. "My relationships have mostly been sour. Couldn't trust them. I told you about my ex-boyfriend, Hugh, and how he lied to me for most of our relationship."

Gianni leaned forward and wiped a drop of sauce from his chin. "You did, but you didn't share the details. I'd like to hear what happened."

Rose envisioned the scene before her. "Well, as I said, he had another girlfriend he claimed was his sister..." Her mind returned to that day two years ago.

Inserting her key into the lock of Hugh's front door, she grinned as she thought about surprising him with his birthday present. Luckily, he'd explained how he had kept his spare key inside his potted plant, trusting her enough to tell her.

Sneaking to his bedroom, she found the door ajar. He was speaking to someone in a soft voice. Slowly opening the door wider, he faced the window with his back to her, talking on the phone. "Oh, Dianne. I love you too, you know that. My work keeps me busy, and I had to travel for my job this weekend. We'll celebrate my birthday a few days later. No harm. Just give me your great surprise in bed. I can't wait to kiss that beautiful naked body of yours from head to toe. I'll do things you can't even imagine." He nodded. "Hmm. Yes, I've loved no one as much as I love you, sweetie. Keep the bed warm. Bye."

Rose clenched her hands, a knotted lump forming in her throat as the room spun around her. She had loved and trusted Hugh, and here he was, cheating on her with another woman.

When he turned around, his face paled. "Rose...I can explain."

She shook her head and hit him hard in the chest. "You bastard. You have a girlfriend and love her more than me? I thought Dianne was your sister. How long have you been cheating?"

"Listen, Rose. I didn't plan for this, but I love you too. This doesn't need to change anything. I'm here for you as well."

She scoffed. "Right. So you're okay with two lovers? How long?"

Hugh stared at his shoes. "Let me explain, Rose."

She dropped to her knees, head bowed, and cried when Hugh put an arm around her. She shoved him away. "How long?"

"We've been together for two years."

She stood up and pushed him so he fell on the bed. "I hate you." She whimpered. "I bet Dianne doesn't even know about me. Does she?"

He shook his head. "No."

"Go rot in hell." She walked out of the door and slammed it behind her.

Rose returned to the present, watching Gianni's eyes flicker as he took her hand and caressed it. "We were together for three years and he'd started his relationship with her after we'd been together for one. Most of our relationship was based on a lie."

"I am so sorry, Rose. That is cold."

She shrugged. "The poor girlfriend too. She was none the wiser. He had a secret life I knew nothing about."

"What happened to that relationship? Have you heard anything since then?"

Rose rubbed the back of her neck, remembering how much it had affected her. "He called me a few months after we broke up and told me that Dianne had left him. That he was now free to get back together with me. She must've found out."

Gianni clenched his hands, swallowing. "What a creep. Why would he think you'd get back with him?"

"He thought his girlfriend was the issue, not realising it was the lies and deceit which were the problem. The bastard only loved himself. Such a damn narcissist."

"Oh, Rose. That must have been hard. You don't deserve anything like that. How do you feel about it now?"

She wiped her mouth with the napkin and sipped her wine. Setting it down, she stared into Gianni's eyes and realised that Hugh couldn't compare to this man before her. He was ten times the man Hugh was. "Funnily enough, I don't feel anything for the man. All the love I felt vanished as soon as I realised what a cheating bastard he was." She devoured the last bit of spaghetti and washed it down with more wine. Further insight revealed that most of her relationships had been based on lies and secrecy. She had never been good enough the way she was and had only attracted men who made her feel insecure and anxious, grieving for the broken relationship each time. But she would usually dive into her career to distract herself from the pain.

Gianni lifted the wine bottle. "More wine?"

She nodded. "Enough about me." He poured more wine, then got up and grabbed the dishes, dropping them into the sink. Opening the fridge, he pulled out a platter of fruit and set it on the table.

He sat back down. "Relationships are hard."

Rose nibbled on a strawberry. "How do you define love?"

He put out his hands. "It's seeing someone across the room and your heart beats so fast you think you might die. It's when your mouth runs dry, you cannot breathe, feeling as if your heart might stop. It's when that person's image flashes through your mind all day, you find it difficult to eat, sleep, drink, and focus on your work, making mistakes. Craving her smile, her voice, her touch, and even her witty comments, her enormous heart, and her love for all things, which is truly gut-wrenching. It's when you yearn for her like your last breath and want to do more than just be friends. You wonder what it would be like to taste her lips or caress her from head to toe and never let her go."

Rose gasped, her hands sweaty as she dropped the strawberry, their eyes meeting and lingering.

CHAPTER 22

It seemed surreal as Rose took Gianni's proffered hand. He pulled her up and slid his hand down her cheek and over her lips. Her body trembled when he drew a strand of hair away from her eyes, leaning into her and feathering her cheeks with his lips, drawing closer to hers by brushing across her chin, forehead, then the corner of her lips. She couldn't breathe and her legs felt numb, especially when his mouth finally met hers, slowly increasing the pressure as his tongue swept around her mouth, tasting her as if he was hungry.

Breaking away from her, he pulled her by the hand and led her to his bedroom. The wine had made her a little tipsy, but she knew exactly what she was doing. Her craving for Gianni had started the first time she met him, and only this moment mattered. Who knew how she would feel once she left Tuscany, but she couldn't think about the future now. She felt swept up in something akin to love in this moment. Or was it actually love?

Rose stood by the bed as he slowly stripped off her blouse and pulled it over her head, then she grabbed Gianni by the shirt and flung it over his head. With his bare chest and her black lacey bra showing, he traced a finger around the centre of her chest and licked his lips, fixating on that area. Slowly, his finger trailed inside her bra, touching the outside of her breast until he reached her nipple. He did the same to her other breast, as Rose closed her eyes and moistened her lips. She hooked a finger into the button of his jeans.

Gianni pulled off his pants and lay her gently on the bed as he slid off her skirt, their bodies meshed while resting on top of her. Kissing her hungrily, he caressed her breasts again, sending those electrical jolts through her body. She lost awareness of her surroundings as she focused on his hot hands and sweeping tongue that pulled her into a world of adrenaline. "You are so beautiful, Rose."

She beamed. "Oh, Gianni. Make love to me." Her nervous laughter led to his reassuring smile, with a fluttery sensation in her stomach. Rose had no problem having one-night stands, so why was it so hard for her to get to the next step?

Gianni unclipped her bra as she lifted her body up for easy access, then rubbed a tender hand over her breast. He inched forward and licked a nipple as she pressed his head into her chest, closing her eyes and moaning. Her hand glided down his penis, over his underwear, and his own sounds of arousal turned her on even more. He wasn't close enough, even when he trailed a hand between her thighs over her underwear. Slowly, he inserted a finger inside her panties and found the sweet spot, probing and prodding gently as she arched her back and licked her lips again. *Oh, hell!* She had never felt such love or arousal before. Not even with Hugh.

Rose felt the firmness of his penis as he pushed it harder against her hand. He kissed her more intensely in the centre of her chest until he was trailing kisses across her abdomen and around her belly button. Every part of her body felt like it would melt as he drew a hand around her inner thighs, reaching for her undergarment, pushing it down her legs and off her body. He moved up, reached for a condom inside the pocket of his jeans, and pulled off his underpants.

Gianni moved back on top, inserting two fingers inside her. "Come for me, Rose." She was so hot and wet, she couldn't help her arousal as he dived deep into her mouth again and moved his fingers in a circular motion. He swept his tongue over her lips and gently bit her bottom one. She cried out in bliss and drew his head into her chest as if satiated. He'd thought about her needs first, but he needed to climax too.

As if reading her thoughts, he stared hard into her eyes as he tenderly guided his manhood inside her, moving into a gentle rhythm. Rose wrapped her legs tighter around him as she writhed and moaned while he pumped into her even faster, their bodies sweating as they increased the pace. Not long after, Gianni came, and Rose screamed in joy.

Gianni leaned on his elbow in bed and stared at Rose, sleeping like an angel. Last night had been the best time he'd ever had with a woman—the way their bodies melded together so easily. Rose knew all the right places to touch him. But it wasn't only the physical arousal that spurred him on; it was something deeper that he couldn't explain. As if their souls had touched and would forever be joined. Was he falling in love with her?

The sheets entangled her smooth, tanned legs and the sight of her exposed breasts aroused him again. She shifted with a smile on her face, as if she was having a pleasant dream. Her palm lay sprawled over his own leg.

All he knew was that he'd never felt this way about any of his ex-girlfriends before. He knew he had sabotaged those relationships. But when Rose spoke about Hugh, he couldn't help but feel guilty. She didn't know how wealthy he was, but why should that matter? He wanted her to care about him for him and not for the money he made. Surely, in time, he would explain how his career had made him a billionaire. Money wasn't important in the grand scheme of things.

Rose stirred and slowly opened her eyes. That tongue of hers wrapped over her bottom lip and he wanted to pounce on her again, feeling himself go hard. "Hey."

Gianni feathered a finger over her nose. "Hey you."

Rose was about to get up when he pushed her back down. "What are you doing?"

"This." He inched forward and smashed his lips hungrily against hers, then pulled away. "How about a shower?"

She grinned. "All right." Rose pulled the sheets off her and hid her breasts with her hands as if shy. Following him to the bathroom, he turned on the tap and faced her. She joined him in the shower, appearing to enjoy the warm spray of water over her shoulders.

Gianni grabbed the soap and washed the centre of her chest and around her breasts as Rose gave in to his touches, especially when he brought the soap down to her inner thighs and washed thoroughly. She flicked her head back and took deep breaths as the warmth of his hands aroused her again. But then he stopped to wash the rest of her body, sensing how close she was to coming again.

He pushed her against the glass of the shower and spread her legs out. Kneeling, he propped his head between her thighs and placed his lips over her mound while holding her buttocks. Rose pushed his head further inside her, as if relishing the rotation of his tongue. He gripped her ass tight; he couldn't get enough of her. *My god!* This woman was undoing him as his adrenaline increased and the sensation made her come.

He smiled, then shifted to stand and kissed her hard, teasing her lips. She reciprocated by kneeling and taking his hardness inside her mouth, tasting him as he held out from climaxing and savoured the tender glide of her lips as he closed his eyes, breathing hard. When he was close to climaxing, he drew her mouth away as his semen poured out. She lifted herself up and fell into his embrace.

A few minutes later, he inserted his manhood inside her and moved with her hard and fast until they shared their bliss and heightened the sensation of the cleansing water falling over them. Would he ever get enough of her?

Magical.

CHAPTER 23

That morning, Rose dug into scrambled eggs, enjoying the pepper and herb flavours as she chewed while watching Gianni stare without eating his own eggs. The intense expression on his face made her wonder what he was thinking. Intermittently, he'd have this dark shadow in his eyes as if he was holding something back. What was on his mind? Was he regretting their love-making last night and earlier that morning? Should she be leaving his house?

It was Sunday, and she had no plans, other than a shopping trip with Luna that afternoon. But she also wanted to research how to start a writer's guesthouse and retreat, and consider how to hire a manager. She would learn to work with her manager from Melbourne. It was a gigantic step to take, and one she couldn't imagine.

As much as she loved life in Italy, she loved her life in Melbourne too. Her mother and friends lived there.

Perhaps another time she'd have a proper vacation and visit her family in southern Italy, and bring her mother along. She deserved to return to her roots and find happiness in her old life.

"Penny for your thoughts," said Gianni.

Rose put down her fork and lay two fingers underneath her chin. She couldn't tell him what was on her mind when a part of her wanted to be with Gianni every day. Now that she'd had a taste of him, how would she feel when it was time to leave? "What are your plans for today?"

His eyes darkened. "I have to work in my business. I rarely work Sundays, but there are a few things I'm behind on." He cleared his throat. "We're building a complex of shops, hotels and apartments, a luxury boutique hotel, and a retirement village, all within the same area. An enormous project which'll keep us busy for years to come."

She nodded. "Sounds amazing. Where's the location?"

"Around the Chianti area."

Rose leaned forward and drank down her espresso. She arched a brow. "Won't new buildings interfere with the beauty of the landscape in these rural areas?"

He shook his head. "No, it's vacant land that is wasted without being used for anything, not even for wine. The location is perfect to draw in more tourists and will give

Italians a lot of jobs." He angled his head. "Have you made a final decision about the villa?"

Rose put a hand over her heart, surprised by the change of subject. Her stomach tightened. "I'm sorry, Gianni. I know it was your project, but I can't sell it. It's my legacy and a way to honour my great aunt, who loved the villa. I can't imagine it being torn down for a set of apartments. We can still renovate it. It's still mostly in a great condition."

He averted his eyes. "It could be lucrative for you. Not having to worry about money for a long time if you sell it." He sighed. "I could show you the numbers and you can make an informed decision."

Rose swallowed, wondering why he wouldn't accept her decision. "I don't care about the money, Gianni. A part of me feels that having these buildings torn down just ruins the natural landscape of these beautiful cities. No wonder we have so many earthquakes and tragedies. It's because we're always interfering with the land. We should preserve these areas and restore their history."

He focused on her and rubbed the back of his neck. "I hear your side, but it's not reality. Tuscany cannot survive that way, and after all these financial disasters, we have no choice but to bring money into the economy. It's smart business. If the land is not being used for vineyards, then it makes sense to have new buildings by tearing down old ones."

Rose inched forward as she bit the inside of her cheek. "I believe there has to be a balance, and right now, it sounds like a lot of this is happening because of greed."

Gianni stared at his hands. He got up and threw his plate into the sink, leaving Rose's on the table. Spots of colour entered his cheeks. "Rather than just generalising, Rose, why don't you get informed? Not everyone is greedy, and I don't appreciate you putting me in that basket. I thought you knew the real me."

Rose's jaw tightened, and her pulse quickened. "And I don't appreciate you trying to get me to change my mind about selling the villa. Why is it so damn important to you?"

He huffed. "You know what? I don't have to justify myself to you when you're leaving soon anyway, so why do you care what happens to that villa? You couldn't care less if someone wants to gift homes to his children in the perfect location. You only see your side, don't you?"

Rose's breathing shallowed and Gianni paced around the kitchen. He stared out of the window. "That's bullshit, Gianni. I care, but I also care about my history and how it hurts to have a piece of my heart torn down. You wouldn't understand because you're all about the modern age and making a nice profit for yourself. I bet you wouldn't think twice about tearing down someone's farm or ranch to build a block of condominiums either."

He scoffed. "Are you serious right now? Who the hell do you think I am? A vulture? A shark? It's obvious you don't know who I am, so I won't waste my breath trying to explain how we're benefiting the community. You only see one side and you're blind to the opportunities, Rose. I hate how you just generalise and think you know it all. Well, you don't. Not a clue." He gestured widely, throwing his arms out away from his body. "You haven't lived here for ten damn years, so don't profess to know what Tuscany is like now or what it needs."

Beads of sweat lined the back of her neck. "I know enough, and I don't appreciate you trying to change my mind about the villa."

"I can't deal with this right now. You can go home now." He stormed out of the kitchen, climbed the stairs, and didn't look back.

Rose stared after him, lowering her head with a trembling chin. She walked over to the chair and bowed her head, a lone tear streaming down her face. What had just happened? A beautiful night and morning turned into a nightmare, and she couldn't help but feel a deep, empty pit in her stomach. She clutched her waist, nausea setting in, and waited to compose herself before leaving, knowing she'd most likely never see Gianni again.

CHAPTER 24

G ianni stared at the computer in his office. The numbers on the spreadsheet in front of him blurred as he attempted to focus. But his mind flashed to Rose and the pain he'd seen in her eyes just before he left her alone in the kitchen. What was wrong with him? Why had Rose triggered him to the point of anger?

He'd felt like a jerk when he accused her of being naïve in the ways of the Tuscan world, but it was true. A part of him knew she was right, and he started to believe that his billionaire status had to be maintained so he could prove himself to his father. Why couldn't his wealth prove he was a worthy and valuable son? Without selling the villa, he had needed to look into other prime locations for Alfonzo, but his father told him to hold off as Rose might change her mind. He knew she wouldn't, and he admired her for not thinking about the money. She didn't care about wealth, but rather about honouring the people she loved.

But there was still a part of him that wished she would change her mind.

They'd had an amazing night and morning and he'd ruined it by talking about the villa. If he didn't have this need inside him, this approval he craved, he would have left it alone. He wouldn't have questioned her decision about the villa. It was her right to say no, and not his right to convince her to change her mind.

He clicked out of the spreadsheet when Guido and Sergio walked into his office. "Hey guys? What's up?"

Guido sat opposite him. "Are you all right? You look like you haven't slept. Care to share?"

Sergio pulled out a chair by the door and sat beside Guido. "Hey, man. You look like you're about to drop in that chair. What's up?"

Gianni's heart palpitated. "Rose and I had a fight after spending an amazing night together." He explained the details. "Before you say anything, I will apologise. I know I got sensitive about the topic, but my dad was invested in those apartments.

Guido shook his head. "I hear you, but when will you realise that what you've achieved far surpasses any need for your dad's approval? When will you realise that pushing women away when you're scared is not the answer?"

"I'm not pushing anyone away. We had an argument, and we both needed to cool down. No harm in that. It happens."

Sergio intervened. "Right." He rested his hands on his lap. "I know I'm not an expert on relationships, man, but even I know you can't treat a woman that way. If she doesn't want to sell her villa, it's her right. She spent the night with you and soon after you treat her like she's made the wrong decision. Not only that, but you tell her not to have her own opinions and literally call her naïve. You property developers are a greedy bunch. The more you have, the more you want."

"Wow! Is that all?" He shook his head. "Speak for yourself, Sergio. I am not greedy, but there's no harm in me wanting to maintain my success."

Guido inched forward. "Make your father understand that she won't change her mind. That it's pointless to wait until she leaves. You trying to convince her to sell might make her think you're using her."

He nodded. "I am not using her. I..." He huffed. "Guido, I understand your perspective and I'll have a conversation with him. I'll also apologise to Rose, as I know I was insensitive about the topic."

"Does she even know you're a billionaire?" Guido asked.

His chest ached. "No, she doesn't. What's the point if she's about to leave soon, anyway? There's nothing to gain by telling her."

Guido knit his brows. "Why are you starting a relationship based on a lie? She should hear it from you and not from anyone else. I know you've kept a low public profile, but she could still find out, and you'd rather she finds out from you."

He rose. "I can't tell her, Guido. Not yet. She'll just get upset I didn't tell her sooner, but it shouldn't matter. If she likes me for me, then I can tell her later."

"You seriously need a self-esteem check, man," said Sergio.

Gianni chuckled, feeling no joy inside. "My self-esteem is just fine, but I'm out of here. I need to pay Rose a visit." He ignored their surprised looks and headed out the door.

Rose answered the door to the stern look of Gianni. She had just returned from her shopping trip with Luna. "What are you doing here?"

He hesitated. "I came to apologise."

She lifted her chin and forced herself to maintain eye contact when she drew the door open wider, ushering him inside. As she led him to the living room, his eyes darted to the fireplace, the drawn lace curtain, surrounding padded chairs, and blue cotton couch with small pillows draped across it.

Rose sat on a chair while Gianni seated himself on the sofa. He cleared his throat. The silence was thick as she gazed at him fumbling with the buttons of his shirt as he crossed his legs. Shifting to the edge of the couch, he rested an arm over the edge and peered past her.

She yearned to reach out to him and wrap her arms around him, but she still burned with irritation. "So?"

He glanced at her and scraped a hand through his hair. "I am sorry, Rose. I got a bit oversensitive and didn't mean to put you down. You have every right to make your own decision about the villa, and I respect it."

Rose sighed in relief. "And I didn't mean to say you were greedy. I know you have a job to do and have worked hard at the vineyard too. I can't imagine how much stress you have on your shoulders and here I am, making it worse. I'm sorry, too."

"It's fine. I know you were just angry, but you're right. There are greedy developers out there who would do anything for money, but I'm not like that. I don't want you to think I don't have a heart because I do. Too much of one sometimes."

Rose's heart warmed as their eyes locked. "I know you're not greedy. You are the kindest person I know, and you were great with the kids at the winery fun day you held."

"Thanks for saying that." He took a deep breath and so did she.

"How's your father doing?"

Gianni grinned. "Better in fact. I spoke to my mum earlier today, and she mentioned he's feeling better. They're doing more tests and waiting to see if the chemotherapy is working."

"Great news. I know how hard it is to have a father who's sick. It gnaws at your insides and gives you this feeling of dread, but to hear your father's doing well gives me hope for him. It's a process, and time will tell."

"It is, and I'm hopeful. We can only take it one day at a time." He squeezed his hands together. "My father's having a birthday party next week and I'd love for you to come." His heart raced at the idea, but he needed to take a stand against his father, showing him that Rose had the right to decide for herself.

"I don't know, Gianni. Your father might not appreciate having the woman who didn't help his friend there."

He shook his head. "No, I'll make it clear to him that he needs to accept your decision. I want us to make a stand."

Rose's heart skipped a beat, wondering if this was a new step for them. "Can I think about it?"

He waved her over, an expression of yearning on his face. "Sure." He grinned. "Come here."

Rose walked over to the couch and sat beside him, their thighs brushing. With one sweep of her hair, he gave her a heady sensation as she met his gaze and beamed. "Don't you have work?"

He shrugged. "I'm taking the rest of the evening off because someone is so worth it." He smashed his lips on hers and caressed the small of her back. Deepening the kiss, Gianni pulled off her sweater and nuzzled her neck while Rose unbuttoned his shirt and slid her hands over the centre of his chest.

He pushed her onto her back on the couch and stroked her bare chest until he reached a nipple. Bending over her, he sucked on her breast, and continued with the other one while Rose pulled his head hard into her chest. His fingers trailed her mound over her jeans until working to sweep them off her legs. Once they were both naked, his penis rubbed over her vulva, teasing her as his tongue swept inside her mouth, igniting heat in her loins.

She pulled away briefly. "I forgot to tell you last night, but I'm on the pill."

He nodded.

Rose took hold of his manhood, slowly guiding it inside her as he moved in rhythm with her, penetrating her with hunger while holding the sides of her face and staring deeply into her eyes. The way he looked at her suggested he might feel something more, but it could've been his desire talking.

The blissful sensation caused her to dig her nails deep into his buttocks, pushing him further inside her as she made a guttural sound and writhed under him. The sound of his climax led to her own moans until they exhaled and held each other in silence.

CHAPTER 25

Rose scanned the interior as she walked beside Gianni in his father's house where they were going to have dinner. Landscape photographs hung on the wall of the spacious living room, and family portraits showcased images of Gianni alongside his parents. Beamed ceilings with a winding timber staircase, a fireplace with a stack of logs, and bookshelves filled with books on wine-making gave the house a rustic ambience.

Voices resounded and guests roamed. Gianni's mother, Lucia, approached and greeted them from the kitchen. She wiped her hands on her apron and wrapped her arms around Rose. "My Gianni has told me only great things about you. Welcome to our home, carina." She pulled away and threaded her hands through her low bun and dark chestnut hair. Lucia was at the level of Rose's chin in height and was petite and slim.

"Thank you," said Rose. "You have a lovely home. Very cosy." Her hands sweated when she realised others were staring.

Lucia hugged Gianni and gave him a cheeky grin. "Has Gianni introduced you to the family?"

"No, not yet."

She smiled and asked for drinks, then turned to Gianni, who looked around awkwardly as he rubbed his hands together. He introduced Rose to cousins, aunts and uncles, but left the most important family member for last.

Gianni glanced at her before introducing her to his father, Matteo, who had the same mouth and prominent Adam's apple as his son. His curly black hair suited him, but his dark eyes scrutinised her as if he was attempting to figure her out. He had a powerful presence in spite of his fragile-looking physique and stiff posture. Her heart raced and a tingle ran up her spine, as he stared at her. "Father, this is Rose."

He limply shook her hand. "Hmm. Yes, I heard about your great aunt. Condolences."

His tone suggested he wasn't sorry at all, but she pushed his attitude aside. "Thank you. It's been hard, but I've had amazing support."

"Good to hear," he said while averting her eyes. "Excuse me." Matteo hurried away to the kitchen and opened the fridge.

Lucia gave her a reassuring smile. "Do not worry about him, dear. He will get over it. My Matteo is a proud man and set in his ways. I, for one, am happy you agreed to keep the villa. Good for you." Before Rose could reply, Lucia joined her husband in the kitchen and whispered to him with a glare while Matteo was opening a bottle of alcohol.

Rose made small talk with Gianni and three of his cousins as they stood in a circle, barely listening to their conversation. Why had she decided to come here and face rude stares from Matteo? He clearly didn't want her there.

A stocky woman with bright red hair asked, "Are you and Gianni serious, and are you planning to stay in Italy?"

Rose flinched, the room spinning around her. "Aah...."

Gianni interrupted. "Oh, come on, Tina. Cut it out." He turned to Rose. "Just ignore her."

One of his uncles, with broad shoulders and a crooked tooth, came up to her and put a hand on her shoulder. "I must say, this is the first time Gianni's brought a woman out to meet his family. You must be special, but I am curious why you didn't sell." His glare unnerved her. Was he against her for not selling the villa too? Oh, she wished she could crawl under a rock.

"Zio, please. Enough about the villa," said Gianni.

However grateful she was for his support, she had to set things straight. "It's fine, Gianni. I can answer." She calmed her breathing. "Honestly, I am honoured to meet you all, and the reason I didn't want to sell the villa is because it means too much to me. I have so many beautiful memories of my aunt there and it would feel like I'm throwing those memories away by tearing it down. She was like a mother to me, and took care of me when I lived in Tuscany." Steeling herself, she added, "I have plans to do something with the villa as it is."

Matteo walked back in and shook his head, his lips pressed firmly together. He handed a glass of alcohol to his wife, who approached Rose and gave her the glass of champagne. She walked back to the kitchen. It was obvious he didn't want to offer the glass to her personally. Rose realised he hated her as much as the uncle did.

She grabbed the drink and drank down most of it in one gulp. Gianni touched her gently on the small of her back. "It's fine," she said.

"No, it's not. I'll talk to him later about this, but please don't take it personally."

"Didn't you mention your father's friend was meant to come?" asked Rose.

Gianni hesitated. "He said he's coming later." Rose's heart raced at the idea of meeting the man who wanted her to sell the villa. She wished she could leave. But what would that say about her? She wasn't one to give up easily on a challenge, and hopefully, she'd win his father over in time. But then again, why bother when she'd be leaving for Melbourne in a few weeks?

They moved over to a table filled with trays of snacks: antipasto platters, home-made sausages, pickled vegetables, fish fritters, and arancini balls. Picking at a fish fritter, she chewed while others bustled about in the kitchen, heading outside to the courtyard or standing around the sofa. Eventually, she conversed with another cousin while Gianni bantered with an uncle who flailed his arms in the air as he complimented Gianni on a property deal.

Once dinner was ready, Gianni sat beside her at the large rectangular table outside as she gazed out over the mountain backdrop with its shaded green and beige undulations, closely growing trees and ferns, and rustling brush in the light breeze. Smells of herbs and spices, fresh sausages, and strong wines made her hungry as Lucia set down plates of pici pasta in front of the twenty guests.

With her back pressed against the steel chair, her eyes locked on Gianni, who held her hand and rested it on his lap. On her other side was Lucia, who gave her a warm smile.

Gianni whispered, "You look beautiful, Rose. I so want you alone right now. I'm counting down the hours."

She laughed. "Me too." Her eyes flickered over to his father, who glared and shook his head as if he could hear what they were saying. He obviously wasn't keen on their relationship, but for now, she'd savour and appreciate the man she was falling for.

An imposing man wearing a loose-fitting blue sweater and tight black pants approached Gianni's father and greeted him with a touch on the shoulder. "Matteo, great to see you. Sorry I'm late."

"No problem, Alfonzo. Take a seat over there," said Matteo. "Lucia, go grab that extra plate." The man waved to all the guests, including Gianni, until his eyes reached her, and he realised who she was. His expression was unreadable. He took a seat opposite her, next to two cousins.

Lucia nodded, scurried back inside and brought out a fresh plate of pasta, setting it in front of Alfonzo. His salt and pepper hair gave him a distinguished look, and no doubt he would have caught the eyes of many women. "Here you are, Alfonzo."

"Thank you, my dear Lucia. I must say you look even more beautiful each time I see you. What's your secret?"

Lucia blushed and waved him away. "Oh, stop it. What would your late wife think?"

Matteo gave him a cheeky grin. "Yes, Alfonzo. Keep your hands to yourself. That beautiful woman of mine is already spoken for."

Alfonzo laughed and forked a strand of Pici. "I hear you, my friend." He chewed on the pasta while eyeing Rose. "You must be Gianni's friend."

Gianni's shoulders stiffened. "Yes, this is Rose."

She beamed. "Good to meet you." What more could she say? Sorry you can't use our plot of land for your set of apartments, and you'll need to find something else?

His eyes cut into her. "You are beautiful, Rose. If I was twenty years younger...." Rose blushed and looked at Gianni, whose face had paled.

"Alfonzo, please," said Gianni.

The tall man shrugged as he wiped his chin with a napkin while others spoke amongst themselves. "Why can't I admire a beautiful woman? Is she taken?"

Gianni clenched his hands. He ignored the man and turned to his uncle beside him. "Tell me about the abandoned property you mentioned, Zio."

Rose lowered her head, her neck appearing to shrink as she bit into the pasta and washed it down with a dry red, apparently having learned to appreciate the taste of dry wine. Her stomach churned and a painful tightness in her throat made her want to run off. Why didn't Gianni tell Alfonzo she was taken and that they were seeing each other? He answered 'yes' about her being his friend. Was he ashamed of her?

She turned to Lucia. "This is beautiful pasta. Is it homemade?"

Lucia nodded. "Well, of course. I don't believe in the packet pasta. Fresh is best." She sighed. "How are you enjoying Tuscany, Rose?"

She ignored the pain in her heart. "Loving it. The place is bringing back a lot of nice memories. I have missed it. Nothing like fresh food, a glass of wine, and the most amazing view. Great way to wake up in the morning."

"Oh yes," said Lucia. "I love it here, but one day I would love to visit Australia. I didn't know your great aunt, but I am sorry for your loss."

"Thank you." From the corner of her eye she could see Alfonzo staring at her, despite talking to Matteo and the other guests.

A few minutes later, Lucia got up and headed back into the kitchen. The wind brushed Rose's cheek as she chewed the last of her pasta. Wiping her mouth, she felt Gianni's thigh brush her own and his hand slide down to her knee, stroking it gently. But despite her arousal, she got an ache in her chest.

"Are you enjoying staying in the villa?" asked Alfonzo.

She breathed deeply, not wanting to engage in conversation with this man who intimidated her. "Yes, it's a beautiful place. My great aunt loved living there too."

He leaned forward. "What are your plans with the property?"

"I am not sure yet, but I'll figure something out," said Rose. A headache set in as the man stared at her lips, his eyes trailing down to her cleavage. Why had she worn this open-necked blouse? She felt naked.

"I would be happy to show you around Tuscany one day this week. I have some free time from work."

Rose's breath quickened, and her knee bounced. She turned to Gianni, who was still engaged in conversation with his uncle. *Definitely not!*

CHAPTER 26

G ianni heard the words "I'm sorry' coming from Rose. What was she talking about? He turned to her as she pressed her lips together and rubbed her knuckles. He felt her left knee bounce while his hand rested there. What was she nervous about?

Alfonzo eyed her. "Not a problem. I thought I could show you the unique sights that Gianni may not have shown you. I've been everywhere in Tuscany. But give it some thought. I'm sure we'll catch up again before you leave."

He wanted to take Rose out. What the hell for? "Rose is busy teaching, so I doubt she'd find much time."

Alfonzo nodded. "I don't want to steal your girlfriend, Gianni."

"She's not my girlfriend, Alfonzo. We're just friends," he said. As soon as those words slipped out, he wanted to slap himself. They might not have made it official, but they were definitely more than friends and he was falling for her. Still, a part of him didn't want to make it official when she'd be leaving and would no doubt forget about him. It was best not to get too attached.

But the look on Rose's face suggested he was in big trouble. She pulled his hand off her knee and averted her eyes. She shifted in her seat, attempting to move further away from him. "You know what, Alfonzo? I might take you up on your offer. I'd be happy for you to show me around. Why not?

Alfonzo slapped his hands together. "Wonderful." He rummaged into his pants pocket and retrieved a business card. "Call me tomorrow." She nodded.

Gianni clenched his teeth, and his muscles tightened. The burning sensation in his chest was intolerable and flashes in his vision made him queasy. What was wrong with him? If Rose wanted to have another tour guide in Alfonzo, so be it. She was free to do as she wanted. But why did it hurt like hell? Why was Alfonzo gazing at her like she was his last meal? It unnerved him.

Lucia and a few of the aunts returned with a panzanella salad, fresh homemade bread with olive oil, and trays of roasted rosemary chicken and beef.

Gianni grabbed a piece of chicken and some salad, then dived into his meat, not tasting the food as Rose engaged in conversation with Alfonzo and his mother. Why was she avoiding him, acting as if he wasn't present? He needed to fix this, but he couldn't interrupt her conversation.

He shifted closer to her, his leg touching hers, yearning to hold her in his arms. He couldn't be jealous of a man who was as old as his father. They might not have been official, but she wouldn't dare have a sexual relationship with the man, would she? But then he remembered how she'd admitted to having casual one-night stands just to forget about her ex-boyfriend. Would she do that here? She couldn't put Gianni in the same basket. But then again, he hadn't been truthful about his billionaire status either.

His reverie broke when dessert came out, a tiramisu and panettoni with espresso coffee. Biting into the tasty dessert, he looked at Rose, who intermittently glanced at him without saying anything. "Are you okay, Rose?"

She cleared her throat. "Fine."

Rose didn't sound fine, but this wasn't the time to talk. When he drove her home they'd sort it out.

His father clinked on his glass. "Attention everyone. Attention!" His eyes darted to everyone except Rose. He would need to sort that out too. "I would like to thank everyone for coming here tonight to celebrate my success with treatment. I am now cancer-free and could not have done it without your support. I love you all. Let's drink to success and love!"

Everyone drank, reciting, "To success and love!" Gianni turned to Rose, who blushed as if nervous. He couldn't be in love with Rose, could he?

After clearing the dishes and moving the table to the side, music flowed from the loudspeaker. Several family members danced on the concrete ground. Gianni's heart stopped when Alfonzo asked Rose to dance, and she agreed without even looking at him.

Shaking, and his heart aching, he turned to his mother. "Let's dance, Mum."

"I would love to, my son." As they stepped in time to the music, he stared over at Rose and Alfonzo, whose arm was around the small of her back. She threw her head back in laughter, and in his distraction, Gianni's foot accidentally bumped into a potted plant. "Damn." He cursed to himself, his foot aching. He stopped dancing.

"Are you all right?" asked Rose.

He nodded. "I'm going inside. I'll put cream on my toe."

"Do you need help?" his mother asked.

"No, stay. I'll be fine." He rushed inside to avoid seeing Rose swoon over a man old enough to be her father.

Once he entered his parent's ensuite, he opened a drawer roughly, found anti-inflammatory cream, then slammed the drawer closed. His pulse raced and his heartbeat pounded. Heat flushed through his body.

Sitting on the edge of his parents' bed, he rubbed the cream over his big toe and struggled to shut out the images of her dancing with Alfonzo. Why did he care? If she wanted to cheapen herself and sleep with a man she barely knew, it was her choice.

Footsteps sounded nearby and his eyes darted in that direction. Rose approached. "How is it?"

He kept rubbing. "I'll survive."

"Can I help?"

He scoffed. "I think you've done enough." Deep breaths from Rose made him think she wasn't impressed, but at this point, he didn't care. She was free to do as she liked.

"What's going on?" Rose asked as she approached him, still keeping her distance. Her gaze ping-ponged, avoiding direct eye contact, and her lips pressed together in a slight grimace. She opened and closed her mouth as if struggling to say what was on her mind. Even the tone in her voice sounded flat.

"Why are you so chummy with Alfonzo? He's probably cosying up to you so you can change your mind about the villa. Don't you realise he's using you?"

Rose hesitated, knitting her brows. "I'm not changing my mind about the villa. If he is, then I'll get a free tour guide. No harm in that."

"He'll try to get into your pants, don't you know that? He's a player. Even when his wife was alive, he cheated on her with younger women."

She shrugged. "Why are you telling me this?"

He put the cap back on the cream and threw it on the bed. "Isn't it obvious? If you plan to have sex with the man, he'll spit you out like he has those other women. You deserve better than that."

"Hmm. Do I?" He frowned, angling his head. Why would she say such a thing? Her posture shifted. "Why didn't you tell Alfonzo that you and I are more than friends?"

Oh, no! How could he be tactful without hurting her feelings? Gianni crossed his arms over his chest and blinked rapidly. "I didn't think it was any of his business, and we *are* friends. We're not an official couple, Rose, and you'll be leaving in a few weeks. What then? A bit of harmless fun is just that—fun. We can still go out and enjoy each other, but this isn't a permanent thing. You know that."

Rose squeezed her hands tight and lowered her head. "You're right, Gianni. I can have amazing sex with Alfonzo. Like you said, we're not an official couple. Not boyfriend and girlfriend, so why not? I love sex with men, and I don't mind a good, erotic one-night stand. I wouldn't mind trying out what it's like to have sex with an older man. See if he still has it." She laughed. "See you later." With a toss of her head, she walked away.

Gianni stared after her, his lungs constricted. He bowed his head over his hands and felt like time had stopped. Why the hell did he feel broken inside?

CHAPTER 27

Rose sat in her kitchen a week later, biting into a chicken schnitzel sandwich, wiping crumbs off her chin. She thought about Gianni, who gave her mixed signals. In one moment, he rejected her while at another he played the jealous boyfriend. Why couldn't he decide? Did he want her or not?

She got the sense he was hiding something from her. At times he'd peer past her, in his own world, with a fleeting darkness in his eyes. Was he going to miss her or was something else on his mind?

Rose realised the relationship was doomed when she knew for certain that she'd be leaving for home. It wasn't like theirs could be an easy commute by plane to the other side of the world.

Devouring the rest of her sandwich, she opened her laptop on the table, searched for any writer's retreats in the area, and found one in Val d'Orcia. It offered all meals for a day, writing classes, cooking classes, wine tasting or tours, transportation, and accommodation. How would she compete with this one? Pricing for one. She would not be charging as high a price, but she had to offer more as a new business. Writing classes for one. She could teach and give guests the space to write and workshop each other's work. If she ever made up with Gianni, he could help restore the place, given his property knowledge. Luna could check on those with medical issues.

As she searched for other retreats, she found a women's one but stopped when her doorbell rang. Was it Gianni? With a spring in her step, she opened the door and winced. *Alfonzo*. She realised it had been a week since she'd met the man and hadn't called him when she said she would.

"This is a surprise. I won't ask how you know where I live."

He grinned. "Can I come in?"

She hesitated, wondering what she'd gotten herself into. "Okay."

The man sat on the couch and crossed his legs, his eyes glancing around the room. "It is still in great condition. The fireplace, furnished windows, well-restored furniture. I can understand why you didn't want to sell."

Rose stood over him. "Yes. Can I get you a drink?"

He nodded. "A glass of water is fine. Iced if you have it."

She headed into the kitchen and reached for a glass from the cupboard, retrieved the jug of water from the fridge, and poured it into the glass. Walking back to the living room, she handed him his glass, then sat opposite on the grey padded chair. "I am sorry I'm not selling. What are your plans with the apartments now?"

He chuckled. "Funny you should ask, but I was hoping you'd change your mind. I understand you're not leaving for a couple of weeks, so we still have time to wait."

Rose's heart constricted. She knew he had a reason for coming by unannounced. "I see." She clenched her hands and crossed her legs. "I won't change my mind, Alfonzo. I have plans to start up a guesthouse and run writers' retreats. As an author myself, I know how much struggling writers need collective support, so that's my plan for the villa."

Alfonzo's eyes darkened and his nostrils flared. "Right. So, nothing I say will convince you otherwise?"

"I'm afraid not. But Gianni's a property developer, so I'm sure he'll find you something just as grand in the area."

"Possibly," he said. "How about I take you out sightseeing? I'm sure there are places you haven't visited which will astound you."

"No thanks. I appreciate the thought, and again, I am sorry about the villa. I hope you understand it's not something I can do."

He fidgeted. "Do you plan to stay here or run the guesthouse from Australia?"

She shrugged. "I can get someone to manage it for me. I don't need to be here, apart from occasional visits."

"And what about you and Gianni? Are you a thing?"

Rose hesitated. What business was it of his? Could she dodge the question? "Listen, I have a few things to do today, so..."

He rose and put the glass on the coffee table. "I understand. I will leave you, but first, about Gianni." Her heart raced. "He is not who you think he is. He's a very private person, so you might not realise who he truly is."

"What are you talking about?"

He grinned, nearing her. "Never mind. Ignore me." Quickly, he leaned in and smashed his lips against hers before she could stop him. Pulling away, she slapped him hard across the face.

"How dare you? Get out."

Pressing his lips together, he lifted a hand. "My apologies. I thought you were interested, but I must have misunderstood. If you change your mind, my bed is empty at the moment." He winked.

Rose could barely breathe as her muscles quivered and her heartbeat pounded. She pointed to the door. "Please leave."

"Good luck, Rose. But ask yourself one thing: Why is Gianni really going out with you?" He grimaced. "I will see myself out." He strolled to the front door and stepped out.

Rose got her breath back when the door closed behind him. Her hands were shaking as she realised she may have led him on at Matteo's celebration. This was her fault, and she hated herself for letting him inside.

Back in the kitchen, she realised that Gianni wasn't the type of man to play games. He had a heart.

Her laptop chimed, bringing her out of her reverie. It was a Facetime call from her friend, Dalia. She answered the call and plastered a smile on her face. "Hi Dalia. How are you?"

"I'm good. How's the land of dreams?"

She laughed. "Amazing. Where's Gina?"

"She has a family celebration today, so I thought I'd check in. You don't look so good. What's going on?"

Rose sighed, thinking she could hide nothing from her friend. But she couldn't mention the kiss when she had a lot of other important things to tell her. "Nothing. Just tired from my writing classes, sightseeing, and…"

"And what?"

"Well, Gianni and I have been kind of seeing each other. We had an argument, but I'm hoping we can sort it out." *He's great in bed too.*

Dalia's eyes lit up. "Wow. Oh, wow. Why didn't you tell me sooner, and how long has that been going on for?"

"Not long, but I'm leaving in a couple of weeks, so we won't see each other after that. It is what it is, Dals. How's Luca? Still giving you headaches?"

"Oh, sometimes. He still struggles to let go of work at times, but he is a billionaire, so I can understand he has responsibilities."

"Yes, so true. If you want him to keep making the big bucks, he'll need to sacrifice his time with you. He's accountable for the graphic design business." She breathed out. "It is nice to have all that money, but a curse too."

"Yes, but enough about me. Tell me about Gianni. Do you love him?"

Rose's heart stopped. "What? I don't think so. No." Was she lying to herself? "I don't know. Maybe. Oh, I'm so confused."

"Rose, it must be hard to feel like that and have to leave him. Would he consider coming to Australia?"

She shook her head. "Impossible. He has responsibilities here, more than I have in Melbourne. Besides, he doesn't feel that way about me. He's accepted that I'm leaving and hasn't asked me to stay. It's not like he's fighting for me, and I don't blame him. His life is here, and my life is in Melbourne."

"Sure, but there can be a compromise. I'm sure he cares about you, Rose, more than you think. What's not to love?"

"Thanks, Dals. But enough about that." She rubbed the palms of her hands together, which were sweating. "I'm planning to run creative writing retreats for writers here. I've done my research and know they work well based on a few other retreats in Tuscany. I can be competitive and lower my prices just to get business."

"That sounds amazing, but wouldn't you need to stay there to run it?"

"Not necessarily. I can find someone to manage it for me."

"Right. Sure. But it won't be easy doing it that way. You'll need to find someone you can trust and who doesn't have many other responsibilities."

Rose wondered if her idea was realistic. Could she have the guesthouse managed from Australia or was it a fantasy?

CHAPTER 28

"It is crazy the way she cosied up with Alfonzo. A disgrace," Matteo said.

Gianni's throat burned. "She was being friendly. Nothing more to it."

His father scoffed as he paced the floor of Gianni's office and held his hands across his chest. "Well, I'll have you know, Alfonzo saw her at the villa today, intending to take her sightseeing."

Gianni hadn't been in touch with Rose for a week, thinking she might need more space after their argument. But he couldn't shake his guilt at not getting in touch sooner. He had hardly slept lately. "Right. Well, I'm tired of you putting Rose down because she didn't do what you wanted. It's her right to keep the villa when she has other plans for it."

"I am not giving up. Hopefully, Alfonzo will help change her mind."

Gianni abruptly rose from the ergonomic chair. He approached his father, who stood by the window with a smug look on his face. "Are you serious right now?" How could he judge her without truly getting to know Rose? "It's cruel to put Rose in that position, and I won't stand for it."

Matteo chuckled. "You won't stand for it? It's already being done, and no doubt Rose will soon give in. He's a man who knows how to charm a woman."

Gianni couldn't believe his father would stoop so low. His heart burned with fury. "Rose won't fall for his damn lies, and I won't let you patronise her this way." He clenched his fists, glaring at his father. "I have been working all night for the past few weeks, trying to find a better piece of land for Alfonzo, and I found one near Montepulciano. I'm waiting to hear from the landowner."

"Don't bother. He's hoping to change her mind by the end of the day."

Gianni wiped his brow then rubbed the back of his neck, taking deep breaths as he fought back on telling his father what he thought about him. The way they were using Rose was under-handed and plain cruel. He had to fix this. "You know what, father?"

"What is it?"

He dived in and decided to be an open book with him for the first time in his life. He was sick and tired of being pushed around. The way he felt about Rose gave him the courage to speak out. "I thought this cancer scare would have taught you something about morals, scruples, but you still haven't changed." He avoided his eyes. "You're still the type of man who needs to lie and cheat to get what he wants and doesn't care who gets hurt."

Matteo flinched. "I did what I had to do to provide for my family. Nothing more to it."

Gianni shook his head. "No, you did it because you're selfish and arrogant, and think the world revolves around you. You did it to manipulate and have control. Even with my success, you think it had to do with you. But I worked hard on my own merits."

His father waved his arms in the air. "That is ludicrous, my son. If it wasn't for the Abbate name, you never would have become a figurehead in the property development world."

He gasped. "There you go again, manipulating your way into my success. Why can't you acknowledge how hard I've worked and that my success is about that, nothing more? But it's been the same all my life. You had your head in business while I was growing up and pushed me aside just so you could make money. Forgot about your son who needed you growing up, who struggled to make friends at school, who wanted you to see him succeed in school plays and at award nights. A son who wanted you to be there when he had secured a scholarship to university. A son who needed to talk to his father after bullies beat him up. You were always too busy, so I had to handle it on my own." He sighed. "I must admit, my uncles were more like fathers to me than you were, and it still hurts that you cannot acknowledge my success because of my business acumen, smarts, or my blood, sweat, and tears. I can never get your approval for anything I do, and I'm tired of it." His father's face paled. "I will not let you hurt Rose the same way you hurt me by discarding her like a piece of rubbish. Like she isn't important and can't make her own decisions. Like she has to be manipulated. I won't let you treat her like that when I..." He knew it without a doubt. "I love Rose, and I won't let you hurt her like that. I'm done with you overpowering me. I am so done." He pushed aside a stack of documents on his desk, reached into a drawer to grab his keys and then slammed it shut.

His father approached him by the desk. "Gianni. This is ridiculous. I have always loved you. Never doubt that. This infatuation with Rose is just that. Nothing more, nothing less. You hardly know the woman."

Gianni scoffed. "Oh, no. I love her. Of that, I am certain." He dangled the keys in his hand. "As for your love, you only loved me when it suited you. Conditionally. You never appreciated me as me and always had to mould me into something you wanted. Well, no more, father." He blew out a huge breath. "I am putting a stop to this right now." He stormed out without turning back.

Gianni walked down the path to Rose's villa and sighed in relief at not seeing Alfonzo's car. With heavy footsteps, he rang the doorbell, knowing he needed to be upfront about everything.

The door swung open, and Rose frowned at seeing him. "What are you doing here, Gianni? Aren't you supposed to be working?"

He nodded. "I had to see you. We need to talk."

She swallowed. "Come in." Rubbing her hands, she led him to the couch in the living room and sat on the edge of it with her feet tucked underneath her legs. He joined her on the couch and wrapped his arms around her, but she stiffened. When they pulled apart, he leaned in to kiss her, but she moved her head, so he kissed her cheek instead.

He looked up at her, darkness in his eyes. "I'm sorry for the other day. I acted... I was out of line and didn't mean to upset you. I might have been a bit jealous."

She tilted her head. "Of Alfonzo?" He nodded. *Wow! So, he did care?* "He was friendly, but I am not interested in a man who wanted to tear down my villa. I'll never see him again."

"But you accepted his invitation, then what you said about wanting to try an older man. I didn't think it was you speaking, so I know I hurt you. I am sorry."

"Whatever, Gianni," she said.

His heart pounded. Despite their argument, something else wasn't right. Had she already seen Alfonzo? "What's going on?"

"I don't know, Gianni. You tell me."

He angled his head. "Something happened. Was it Alfonzo? Was he here?"

Rose took a deep breath and got up from the couch. She stood up with her hands on her hips and stared down at the ground. "Yes, he was here."

His heart skipped a beat, and he wondered what the man said to make her distance herself like this. "What happened? Did he upset you?"

She laughed. "Funny you should say that Gianni. Tell me. Were you using me just to get me to sell the villa?" She averted her eyes, her body shaking. Then she approached the fireplace and stood against it, as if needing to distance herself further.

His throat felt parched. "Listen. I must admit that, initially, I was hoping you'd sell the villa, but when I got to know you, I realised you had made your decision and I respected that."

"Right. So the fact that your father and Alfonzo had a deadline didn't factor into it. You knew they were waiting until I was close to leaving, didn't you?"

He felt like a piece of shit. Why couldn't he be upfront with her from the start? "Yes, I did, but I didn't agree with it. I told them you had plans for the villa and wouldn't change your mind."

"Yet you wined and dined me without telling me there was this deadline. Without telling me that Alfonzo was most likely using me."

"Come on, Rose. You knew who he was and chose to dance with him at the party."

Wiping her palms, she fidgeted and turned her back to him. She picked up the photo of her great aunt and placed it against her chest. "I was only being friendly, and you hurt me when you... I mean, you weren't forthcoming about us at the party, so I got mad. You know this, so I won't rehash it. But don't turn this around on me. You weren't honest with me, and even now, I'm sure you're still using me, hoping I'll change my mind."

"That's ridiculous, Rose. You know I support your plans for the villa, and if you want to turn it into a guesthouse, I can make that happen. I'm a developer."

"Hmm. About that." She cleared her throat and put the photo back on the mantelpiece. "Alfonzo mentioned you're not who you say you are. What did he mean by that?"

Gianni's head spun. *Christ!* He didn't want her learning about him this way. Another thing he should have been honest about. But he had planned to tell her today, wanting her to hear it from him. "Rose, you need to understand I didn't tell you for my own reasons. I didn't think it was relevant, seeing as you'll be leaving Italy soon. I wasn't sure where we were going with our relationship."

She pursed her lips and clenched her hands, which lay at her side. "Just spill it."

Gianni took a calming breath, desperately wanting to reach out to her and show her how much he loved her. "Rose, I... I am a....billionaire." He didn't like the way her head fell into her chest or how she refused to look him in the eyes. She walked to the front door and opened it.

"Get out." She avoided his eyes and scratched her palm.

He got up and touched her gently on the shoulder, but she shoved him away. "Rose, please let me explain. I didn't tell you because I wanted you to get to know me as me and not by the amount of money I have. It has no relevance to how I feel about you."

"I said, get out. I can't look at you right now."

"Rose, please. I love you."

Her eyes softened for a fleeting moment, but soon hardened. She exhaled and glared at him. "You love me? Right. You don't know the meaning of the word." She shook her head. "We are so done, Gianni. You're just a typical greedy rich guy. I'm not surprised."

He stepped outside and turned back around, but she had already slammed the door closed. Gianni stared at it, hoping she would open it, but she never did.

As he walked to his car everything seemed surreal. He slid into the driver's seat, bowed over the steering wheel, and allowed himself to feel the ache in his chest and the burn in this throat. He deserved nothing less.

CHAPTER 29

Gianni and Guido rested back against the sofa as they sipped beer and watched a game of football on TV three days later. Gianni's head wobbled from heavy drinking and the pain in his heart dulled. He rarely drank himself stupid over a woman, but it was different this time. He'd never been in love before.

Guido clinked his bottle against Gianni's. "To not falling in love."

Gianni nodded, throwing back his head and laughing. "I'll drink to that, man." He lay back against the couch, seeing Rose's beautiful image in his mind, and shook it out. Could he fix it? She might have broken up with him, but he'd give her a few days to cool down, then she'd come around and realise that he hadn't meant to hurt her.

But then what would be the point when she'd be leaving for Melbourne in a week? There was no way they could stay in a relationship from one end of the world to another.

Despite that, they still had time to fix things between them. They'd need closure, at least.

Guido shoved him on the shoulder. "Earth to Gianni."

He broke out of his reverie. "Sorry, what?"

"I said, what are you going to do about Rose? Are you going to talk to her before she leaves or is this it between you two?"

He shrugged. "Not sure. I hurt her by not telling her who I really am. Do you think she'll forgive me?"

Guido leaned forward after resting his bottle on the coffee table, squinting. "Hmm. You could offer her ideas for her guesthouse. Let her know you'll be there to help renovate the villa. If you show you're supporting her and want her to move forward with the place, she'll realise you care about what she wants."

"I guess, but it still doesn't make up for the fact I lied about being a billionaire."

Guido curled a brow, picked up his bottle and took another drink. He wiped his mouth with the back of his hand. "Not directly, but it shows you're willing to put your money to good use and serve the writing community. But also, explain to her why you lied—if she'll listen." He peered into the distance. "Make sure she understands it's because of all your hang-ups with your dad and past relationships. If you get into what was going through your mind at the time, she'll understand. Make her hear you, Gianni. If you love her, don't let her go."

Gianni gripped the bottle, savouring the coldness around his fingers. "But she's leaving. How am I going to cope with her being gone?"

Guido hesitated. "You two will work it out. I'm sure of it. Whatever will happen will happen. Have faith."

"You're right." He stood up and fought back the weakness in his legs. "I'm going to Rose. She's working at the centre today."

Guido waved a hand. "You're drunk and should not be driving."

"I'm going to sober up, drink water and a coffee, then I'll be fine. It has to be today because time is precious, and I don't want to waste it."

Gianni took a calming breath as he stepped inside the building where Rose was teaching and sat down on a chair. He didn't want to interrupt her session, so he would sit and wait another ten minutes until she finished her class.

He'd drunk plenty of water and coffee before feeling sober enough to drive to Montepulciano and beg for forgiveness. Surely, she would relish their last week together before she had to leave. Was it possible that she would stay to run the writing retreat, or would she be managing it remotely? If she could get a manager to run it, she didn't need to be in Tuscany in the beginning stages.

A group of people started walking towards the exit and down the stairs. He waited until Rose showed up, but ten minutes later, she was still a no show. He made his way to the classroom and knocked on the open door so as not to startle her.

Rose was playing with the palms of her hands, her mind distant and her eyes red as if she'd been crying. When she spotted him, she began stacking piles of documents on top of each other. She inserted them into her satchel and remained seated with her hands clasped on the desk. "What do you want?"

"I want to explain. Can I come in?"

She shrugged. "It's a free country."

Gianni stepped inside, pulled over a chair and sat facing her. Her eyes were cast downward and her lips were pressed together as if she didn't want to be here. His heart raced and his hands sweated as he gazed at her, wanting to run his hands through her hair, wanting to take away her pain with a tender embrace. But she wasn't having any of that. "I'm sorry I didn't tell you who I was, Rose. I was worried you wouldn't want me for me and felt you'd leave if I told you the truth. I wanted to savour the time with you, knowing we had little time together."

Rose chuckled. "You could have told me from the start before I...." She shook her head. "Never mind."

He angled his head, wondering what she was about to say. Did she care about him as much as he cared for her? "You're right. I should have told you who I was. I should have been there for the meeting about your villa, but my friend, Sergio, took my place. But after seeing you in Montepulciano on your first day here, I didn't want to mix business with pleasure. I knew it would affect my getting to know you and hated the thought that—"

"That you would use me so I could sell the villa? Try to butter me up? I mean, how do I know you're not here now to get me to change my mind? I've still got a week before I leave."

"No, Rose. I accept your decision, and I never used you. I would have liked you to sell your villa, but it wasn't a desperate situation for me. If you did, great, but if you didn't, I would have respected that."

"Your father has an enormous influence on you, Gianni. I know his approval means a lot to you, but I can't have another man in my life who keeps secrets and lies. I don't know if I can ever trust you."

Gianni's face paled. "What are you saying?"

Rose rubbed her hands across the table, but they were shaking. Averting her eyes, she said, "I can't see you anymore. What's the point, anyway? This can't work."

He swallowed, desperately needing to ease his parched throat. The emptiness in his chest was like nothing he'd ever felt before. No breakup had ever affected him this way. "No, let's talk about this. I am happy to work at your guesthouse with you. I have ideas to improve the villa and build any rooms you need. We can talk about it and make a plan. I can make great use of my money for your project and this community." The darkness in her eyes told him she wouldn't change her mind, but he had to try. "We can work as a team. Maybe when you return, we can, I don't know, try from a distance?"

She scoffed. "Oh, bullshit, Gianni. I'm leaving and that's that." Rose huffed and keeled over as if she was sick.

Gianni rushed over to her and touched her on the back of her neck, his mind racing. Was she sick or hurt? "Rose, talk to me. What's wrong?"

She pulled his hand away. "I'm fine. Just tired, that's all." Swallowing, she fought back tears, and he wanted to wrap his arms around her and tell her he was a jerk and had fallen madly in love with her. But she already knew how he felt.

Rose got up and stared through the window with its strung up holland blind. The sun's glare made her squint, but she kept her back to him. "I don't need your help, and I can't trust you with my project. Besides, I'm rethinking the idea. I don't want to bother anymore. You hurt me. I thought I could trust you, and you lied to me. Kept secrets." She squeezed her hands tight. "You never knew me if you thought I would want your damn money. I have my own." Leering, she added, "I do well, and I've never had to rely on a man for anything."

Gianni approached her slowly. He couldn't lose her, not when he doubted he'd find this kind of love with anyone else. She was it for him. "I was a jerk, Rose. I am sorry for lying to you, but I've developed this pattern of scaring women away. I think I've been scared of commitment because of who I am."

She brushed a tear. "That's still no excuse. I value honesty and trust, and when you didn't tell me, it made you out to be a fraud in my eyes. I don't know who the real Gianni is. Don't you see that?"

"I have never felt worthy of many women, you included. I'd self-sabotage with my ex-girlfriends. I probably didn't tell you who I truly was because I wanted you to stick around. I knew you'd react like this. But then I also had these mixed feelings. You're leaving, Rose, and I don't know what to do with that."

She laughed. "It's funny how you can rationalise your behaviour, but a lie is still a lie. Besides, I have too much in my head right now to think I could ever forgive you. You lied to me about who you truly were. How the hell did I not know that? You're not even on social media. How is that even possible these days?"

Gianni took a calming breath. "Listen, I know it's a lot to take in, but I made mistakes and I'm human. I've grown over these past weeks. Can we talk about this in a couple of days after you've had time to process everything? Please, Rose. Think about it."

Rose rubbed at another tear falling down her cheek. Her breathing seemed erratic, and her hands trembled as she pulled a strand of hair away from her eyes. Scurrying back to her desk, she picked up her satchel and handbag. "I'm done. I don't need time to process, Gianni. I've made my decision." She took a deep breath. "It is what it is."

He pressed a fist to his lips and his shoulders drooped. A painful tightness in his throat prevented him from saying anything. Spots flashed in his vision as Rose headed out of the room and out of his life. How could he let the love of his life leave him?

CHAPTER 30

Gianni leaned over his desk, checking a report about blueprints for his latest property deal in Tuscany. He read through the same phrase three times before it finally sank in. The coffee on his desk remained untouched. His manila folders lay in a disorganised heap on his desk, and pens lay scattered around them.

His body sagged with exhaustion as he hadn't slept the past two days, struggling to focus on his day-to-day tasks. Thankfully, his father was able to fulfil his vineyard duties on a part-time basis, so he could focus more on his own work. Not that it mattered when, with every passing minute, all he could think of was his beloved Rose. Her smile, the way she bit her bottom lip, and the way she scrunched up her nose when she was nervous. Even her voice sent him over the edge.

He had tried to call and text her, but she was ignoring him. In a few days, she'd be leaving, but what could he do?

If she had forgiven him, she would have reached out. But she hadn't. What did he expect after she'd told him they were done?

His reverie broke when his father waltzed in. "Hello, son."

He hadn't forgiven his father for being disrespectful to Rose. "What do *you* want?"

The man opened and closed his mouth as if not knowing how to respond. He raised a brow and sat down. "Alfonzo is pleased with the additional land you found in Montepulciano for the set of apartments," he said while he fiddled with the collar of his shirt. "He even forgives you for not changing Rose's mind about the villa."

Gianni chuckled, his chest burning. "You can tell Alfonzo to shove it where the sun doesn't shine."

Matteo winced. "I beg your pardon, Gianni? After everything that man has done for you, you should be more respectful."

Gianni sighed. "I believe I've thanked him enough for the way he was there when you weren't, growing up." His father's eyes darkened. "But the way he's behaved with Rose—it wasn't right to try and use her that way."

"Oh, come on. He's apologised for the kiss and thought she was amenable to changing her mind. She had mixed feelings about the villa."

A hand flew to his chest, and his posture stiffened. A heavy feeling in his stomach made him sick. "What the hell are you talking about?"

Matteo frowned. "I thought you knew. Alfonzo kissed her when he visited. He's attracted to the woman and wanted to soften her resolve about the villa. He thought he could win her over." Gianni's eyes darkened. "Not that I condone his behaviour. It wasn't right, but I am apologising on his behalf."

Gianni felt like sinking into his chair. Why hadn't Rose told him? Or had she enjoyed the kiss? "Where the hell is he? I need to give him a piece of my mind."

Matteo got up from his desk. "Ludicrous. You will do no such thing. After failing to sell the villa, the least you can do is forget it happened."

Gianni sighed. "Have you not learned anything since the last time we spoke? You both tried to use Rose for your own benefit, and care more about profits than people. I could die tomorrow and you wouldn't give a shit. Hell, you were close to dying and still didn't learn a damn thing about life, about people. How could you be so cold my whole life? You never loved me; you just used me for what you could get." He clenched his teeth. "It's because of your strong influence in my relationships that they have turned to shit. Now Rose hates me because she thought

I preferred money over her. She thought I was using her because of the villa. I acknowledge my sick part in it, but you're worse. You and Alfonzo." He pointed to the door. "Get out of my office."

His father appeared shaken, his eyes turning inward. With a trembling hand, he reached out to his son, who shifted back. "No, Gianni. I've always loved you. I might not have known how to show it, but you were always my son who I was proud of. The only reason I was hard on you was to push you to greater heights. I knew you could achieve so much more. You had potential."

Gianni didn't want to hear it, his fury bypassing the love he had for his father. "Just get out. Now!"

His father surrendered. "Okay, son. I'll let you cool down." With slow steps, he walked out of his office.

Gianni's body quivered as he stared into his hands. Had he turned into his father without realising it? Had he subconsciously pushed the love of his life away?

CHAPTER 31

Rose sat up, her back leaning against the headboard as she pasted on a fake smile while gazing at the screen. "Hey, Dalia. Gina. This is a surprise. I thought you guys were calling me tomorrow."

Gina squared her shoulders. "From your message about wishing you could leave earlier than scheduled, we got the impression that something happened. Are you all right?"

Rose wiped her nose with a tissue. Her chin trembled and her shoulders quaked, sending a chill down her spine. The heaviness in her chest and a need to be alone caused her to wish she could end the call. Her shoulders drooped, and she lacked the energy to feel any more sadness. "Not really." She shed a tear and quickly rubbed it away.

"Oh, Rose," said Gina. "What happened?"

She shrugged, then blurred vision made her blink a few times. "I think I'm in love with Gianni, and I...I don't know what to do about it."

"Does he know?" Dalia asked.

She shook her head. "He hurt me, Dals. I don't know if I can forgive him, but I want to. I so desperately need to. What do I do?"

"Okay, start from the beginning," Gina said. "We cannot advise you with a lack of information. What happened?"

Rose gave them the whole sordid story, noticing their wide eyes and loud sighs. " You see, he's a jerk, and as much as I love him, I hate him too." She waited with bated breath for their advice, and when Dalia moved closer to the screen, she knew it'd be a more positive reply than Gina's.

"You have to talk to him. Sort it out, Rose. Do not leave before speaking to him and explaining how much he hurt you. Tell him that you love him too."

Gina intervened. "The rich only take care of the rich, Rose. I say, start fresh and forget about him. If he truly loved you, he would move heaven and earth to be with you. It sounds like he hasn't made an effort to see you."

"He has called and left text messages over the past couple of days, but I've either ignored him or given curt replies so he would leave me alone." She took a calming breath, fighting to see the screen as she shed more tears.

"Oh, Rose. I wish we could be there with you. I am so sorry. We love you, and we're here for you, whatever you decide," said Dalia.

"I just need to move on and get on with my life—not here."

Dalia nodded. "Maybe a bit of space might do you guys good." She exhaled. "But from what you told us, it sounded to me like his father and Alfonzo pressured him. If you look at it from his perspective, he barely knew you well enough to share his billionaire status at the start. I admit, he made mistakes and could have done things differently, but his mistakes weren't personal. It sounds like he truly cares about you, Rose. Don't let the chance at love pass you by. Try to fix it."

Gina pursed her lips. "Do not make any hasty decisions, Rose, particularly when your home is here, not in Tuscany. It is a relationship that cannot work when you live so far apart from each other anyway. What chance is there?"

Rose chuckled, loving Gina for her reality checks. "You are right. I can't see a future for us when I'm back home. I've even decided not to manage a retreat with the villa. I'll speak to Guido and see if he can find a tenant for me, so I can rent it out. At least for now."

"I wish the retreat could have worked for you. But maybe later, when you've had time to work through your issues with Gianni," said Dalia.

With a new resolve, Rose pulled herself up and sat on the edge of the bed while holding her laptop. "I will send you the flight details, ladies." Her heart felt heavy, and she couldn't talk about him anymore. It was too painful.

"Take care of yourself, and we'll see you soon," said Dalia.

"Yes. We will see you in a few days," said Gina.

Rose started packing, an image of Gianni in her mind. No, she had to get on with things and live her life. Her relationship with Gianni was just a fantasy, a dream in a place that belonged in her past.

But the sight of her phone on the bed made her wonder. She quickly grabbed it, thinking it might not be a bad idea to at least say goodbye. Her heart needed to see him here before she left, despite her head telling her she should leave it be.

Hovering over his number, her finger trembled and her breathing sped up. Pressing on Gianni's number, she called him, but his voicemail came on. *Damn.* She would try him again later.

Gianni raced towards Montepulciano, deciding to take a stand and make Rose listen to him about how much he loved her. He'd tell her he was a jerk who wouldn't give up on her without a fight. Should he have called first? Showing up felt more romantic

His hands sweated on the steering wheel as he passed by slow drivers and trucks. Deciding to pull over, he stopped the car and rummaged in his glove box, but nothing. His phone wasn't there. Gasping, he realised he must have left it charging in his bedroom. He'd been making a lot of mistakes lately: not sleeping, not eating, and was such a nervous wreck at not resolving things with Rose. Nothing he could do about it now. He was too far from home, and he assumed she'd be at the villa, packing.

Getting back on the road, he forged ahead, knowing he was only five minutes away. His heart lifted and his mind ran through scenarios of how she'd wrap her arms around his neck and kiss him like he was the last man on Earth. Even if she lived in Australia, they could make their relationship work somehow. They could work out the logistics later, but he knew in his heart he would never let her go. He could have kicked himself for not trying harder to make her understand, but she needed time and space to process everything. He owed her that, at least.

Parking the car in front of the villa, he wondered where her rental car was. Had she returned it already even though she was only leaving in three days? No doubt she had done that and was home.

Ringing the doorbell, he waited for a few minutes before walking around the side and back of the villa. The home looked dark. *Hell!* He couldn't call her with no phone, and he had no way of knowing where she was.

As he headed back to the front, the sound of the creaking door made him abruptly square his shoulders. Rose stood there wearing a red, flowing dress that enhanced her dark eyes. "Hi, Rose."

"Did you realise I called you?"

"You did?"

She nodded. "I didn't want to leave things in a bad way and thought we could at least say goodbye. Get closure." Her bottom lip trembled. "Come inside."

"No, listen. I want us to take a boat ride where I can explain everything. If you still decide to end things, I'll respect that, Rose. Let's have at least one more day together. As friends." She bit her bottom lip, the longing in her eyes telling him she was considering it. She opened her mouth, then closed it. "Please."

She shifted her feet and stroked her arms, her eyes shining as she gazed at his lips. Her breathing deepened and her hands moved to rubbing the centre of her neck. Rose was clearly nervous and had mixed feelings, but he waited as he leaned in, wanting to wrap his arms around her and tell her that everything would be all right. That he loved her with all his heart and soul. "Fine, Gianni. I'll hear you out."

He hadn't noticed that he'd been holding his breath until he expelled a big gulp of air as he waited for her to get ready.

CHAPTER 32

The heat scorched Rose's face in Porto della Maremma San Rocco where Gianni's boat was docked near other boats. A crowd of men and women headed around nearby boats as she pondered the almost two-hour drive from Montepulciano in silence. Gianni had explained that he wanted to talk seriously once they'd reached Viareggio by boat and to remind her of what Italy had to offer. They could at least spend one final day together before she left.

The boat was impressive with its four, comfortable seats including the driver's, and had a glossy exterior shine with a splash of red over creamy white. The Bimini offered shade from the scorching sun, but the humidity made her sweat.

A bulky middle-aged man with a beard and dishevelled hair waited for them, sporting a broad smile. "Hey, Gianni. I thought you would not make it." He grabbed a piece of rope and looped it around a post to hold the boat steady as they headed inside.

He nodded in greeting towards Rose as she stood awkwardly beside Gianni, a part of her wondering why she'd agreed to this day trip with this man she loved but could never have. She carried a bag with a towel and her thong sandals in it.

Gianni carried his own beach bag. "Sorry, man. The traffic was hell from Montepulciano. You can't imagine."

"Oh, yes I can, but not a worry," he said. The man picked up a plank and threw it to the edge of the pier. Gianni stretched out his arm to offer his hand to help her across it.

Rose waved him away. "I can do it."

His eyes darkened. "This is Rose. Rose, Dario. He's my driver when I can't be bothered steering the boat or when I have guests over."

She nodded. "Pleased to meet you, Dario."

Dario grabbed her hand as she boarded. "Welcome, Rose. It's not often I get to meet a beautiful woman on Gianni's boat. You must be special."

Her stomach tingled as she turned to Gianni, who had red splotches across his neck. Was he embarrassed? "I'm not special, Dario. But thank you for saying that."

She took a seat next to Gianni when Dario eventually started the engine and they sped across the calm sea with blue skies above and a light breeze. The smell of salt permeated her senses as she savoured the smooth motion of the boat. The wind whipped across her cheeks as she stared out over the ocean, loving the calmness of it.

"Listen, I want to explain everything, Rose, but only once we arrive in Viareggio. It's loud on the boat, but this is how magical Italy is."

"It's fine. I'm happy to look at the view and enjoy the sun." She watched him rub his tanned legs beneath loose white shorts and a baggy blue t-shirt, wishing they could enjoy each other one last time. But what was the point? "How long have you had this boat?"

He shrugged. "I've had it for a few years. I come out here when I need a break or to get clear about things, family stuff, that sort of thing. It allows me to think and chill at the same time. It helps."

"Is that why you invited me here? To think?"

Gianni swallowed. "Yes. I know you're leaving in a couple of days, and I wanted to show you a part of my heart, a part of me. This is my life. Not only my work or family, but this." He waved his arms around. "This is a part of who I am, and I hope you can understand that I don't have ill-intent. That I'm a normal person. I wanted you to get to know the real me."

Rose shook her head. "I never said you had ill-intent, Gianni." She pressed her chin into her chest, wanting to push aside her strong feelings for this man.

Gianni changed the subject. "Would you like a bottled water?" She nodded, so he rummaged in his backpack, pulled out a bottle, and handed it to her.

She reached out and he slipped it into her hands, their fingers touching. He kept his there until Rose pulled away. If he was trying to get her to change her mind about their relationship, he was doing an amazing job. But she had to be strong. She'd give him this last chance to talk, purely to get closure and to share one last memory.

Dario and Gianni, who appeared to be close friends, engaged in occasional chatter while the remaining hour and a half was spent in near silence between herself and him.

Turning off the engine, Dario anchored the boat before grabbing Rose's sweaty hand and helping her to disembark. "It was such a pleasure to meet you. I'll see you in a few hours. Enjoy Viareggio."

"Thank you, Dario. I'll see you soon." They made their way across the beach after she slipped on her thongs, following Gianni across the fine sand.

Viareggio was picturesque with its sandy beach, rolling waves along the shore, and a passeggiata, or promenade, that Rose and Gianni walked across in silence. Clouds scattered across the sea-blue sky and boats moved in the distance with the mountainous backdrop behind them. They found a spot to lay their towels and Gianni sat down on his.

Rose breathed in the salty air, holding onto her legs as she sat down beside him, ignoring beachgoers with umbrellas around them. The sun made her squint, so she put on her sunglasses and stared out over the calm blue sea. People were swimming, playing ball, soaking up the sun, and building sandcastles with buckets.

"What do you think?"

She swallowed. "It is beautiful. Magical, really. Thanks for bringing me here." She clasped her hands around her knees. "When I lived here, I never got the chance to travel, especially after my dad got sick."

"I am sorry," Gianni said. "Grief is the worst part of life."

She nodded. "It is. But we can't avoid it, can we? Any kind of loss, whether it's through death or the ending of a relationship."

"I totally agree." The white of his knuckles showed as he gripped his hands tightly together, puffing. Should she say something? "I truly am sorry, Rose."

Her heart went out to him as he picked at a fingernail, his eyes not meeting hers, as if he couldn't look her in the eye. "I know you are."

Taking a deep breath, he stared out over the water. "I never wanted to lie to you about any of it, but at the start, I wanted to make a good impression, so I couldn't tell you about the villa. I was too nervous to talk to you about it, so I got my friend, Sergio, to talk on my behalf. I wanted to get to know you, and didn't want you to think I was pretending to be attracted to you because of the villa. I didn't want to mix business with pleasure." He reached for his backpack and pulled out bottled water, then sipped before wiping his mouth with the back of his hand. "Later, as we got more involved, I didn't want you to think my identity was based on my billionaire status. I wanted you to get to know me for me, and no, I knew you weren't a gold digger. It was never about that; it was more about my father's influence in making me feel like dirt all the time. Never being able to measure up to him, no matter what I achieved. I felt pressured by him to get you to sell the villa, but I never once used you because of it. I liked you for you and respected your decision not to sell." He turned to her briefly. "My father had always pressured me growing up too, so I felt forced to help Alfonzo and him. It took me falling for you to realise that I'm good enough on my own. That I don't need my father's approval. I need to live my own life." He leaned closer. "It's not the Abbate vineyard name that gave me success. It was my business knowledge. My passion for property development." He cleared his throat while Rose briefly turned to him. "As for not telling Alfonzo about our relationship, I knew he'd try to put ideas in your head about me. I didn't want him interfering with that, but I also knew you weren't interested in him that way. I wanted us to be free to have a relationship without the villa hanging over our heads." He clenched his jaw. "But I must admit, I was scared. Scared to commit...and worried that I wasn't good enough for you. In all my relationships, I'd always sabotage them because I didn't trust in their strength. I felt like nobody understood me, so I made sure I gave them a reason to leave, or I'd leave them before they could leave me. I just felt misunderstood, like I didn't have a voice when my financial status overrode who I truly was on the inside. I lacked a true connection with my ex, despite loving her. But I pushed her into the arms of someone else. I honestly didn't want you to see me as being wealthy because that had always meant I wasn't seen as the real Gianni, who loves, cares, and has a heart. I am more than my wealth and status. Know that."

She nodded. "I wouldn't have seen you that way," said Rose.

He angled his head. "Yes, but in the bigger scheme of things, having that success doesn't mean anything if I couldn't measure up to you in terms of who I was as a person. Whether I was a good enough person to be with you. I wanted you to see *me*."

"Come on, Gianni. If anything, I didn't feel I was good enough for you. Keeping secrets was what my ex-boyfriend did, and you're the complete opposite."

"I'm sorry. I never meant to hurt you." He reached for her hand, and she let him hold it. "I have missed you. So much. Do you forgive me?"

The time since Gianni had confronted her at the writing centre had been hellish. Over that time she had barely slept and couldn't eat. She was sure she'd lost weight. She'd missed him like crazy, and loved him, but it wasn't enough. In a couple of days, her life would return to normal in Melbourne, and she would have to put Gianni behind her. "Yes, I forgive you, but it's not enough, Gianni. My life isn't here. It's in Australia."

He let go of her hand and leaned back on his towel. "Can't we make it work?"

She lowered her head, her neck appearing to shrink. Why did she feel dizzy, as if she was losing her breath and sense of reality? Shifting closer to Gianni, she let the tears fall. "I am sorry." She picked up his trembling hand, leaned into him, and wrapped her arms around him. The touch of their bodies comforted her but made her sick too, knowing that she would never see him again. It was too much to bear when she couldn't see it working out. How could they have a long-distance relationship?

Pulling away, Gianni brushed her tears away with his fingertip, their eyes lingering. "We have two different lives. We're from different worlds," said Rose.

He nodded. "You're right. It could never work when I can never leave my life here and you could never leave yours. I'm sure that once you get back to reality, you'll realise that this thing we had was just a fantasy. Not practical." He averted his eyes and swallowed hard. "I have a lot of growing up to do, and you deserve someone who can be there for you, always. I've got too much baggage."

Rose couldn't breathe and clutched at her stomach. Why didn't he fight for her? He might change her mind because of her mixed feelings about them, but he gave up. "I guess that's it." Her voice choked with tears as she pulled her knees up and pinched hard at her skin. The weakness in her legs made her rub them roughly, as if she could bring them life. She wanted to cry but couldn't do it here with Gianni around. Abruptly, she got up. "I need to go to the bathroom. Give me a few minutes." He nodded, his expression darkening.

She trudged over the sand, reached the toilet block, and leaned forward, tears dropping down her cheeks as she cried with all her strength. Ignoring passers-by, she buried her face in her hands and let it all out.

CHAPTER 33

E arly the next morning, Rose sipped on a café latte with Luna in Montepulciano. People strolled along the sloping cobblestone walkway as her thoughts turned to Gianni. If only he had fought for her. But then again, what did she expect when she was the one who had said that it could never work?

Luna patted her on the shoulder. "Earth to Rose?"

She put down her cup and looked across at her friend. "Hmm?"

"I wanted to know what happened on Gianni's boat. I need details. What the hell's going on between you two?"

Rose shrugged, resting back against her seat. Her chest ached from how she had cried her heart out. She and Gianni had ventured back to his boat in silence. It was as if they'd both been to a funeral; it was that morbid. Poor Dario attempted to lighten the mood, but it was like trying to cut a piece of brick.

She recounted their visit to the beach, with Luna's eyes dilating. "I hated him for what he did, and that ruined things. But then he didn't fight for us in the end."

"Come on, girl. What did you expect? You rejected him, so he did the only thing he could do." Rose gave her a curious stare. "He went into survival mode, believing he could do without you, but I've seen him around you. He's totally in love with you, girl."

"Survival mode?"

Luna threaded her hands through her hair after drinking from her espresso. "Self-protection by trying to convince himself that your relationship was a fantasy. He's pushing his emotions so far down that he thinks he can just move on."

She nodded. "You might be right. But how can we make it work? Neither of us will make that sacrifice."

Luna frowned. "What about the writer's retreat? Couldn't that be a way to stay here if you choose?"

"A pipedream, Luna. I don't have the motivation to even try. Even Gianni said we were only a fantasy." Rose placed a hand over her heart, feeling it constrict. She couldn't get the image of his face out of her mind. The way his Adam's apple shifted when he was nervous, and the way his curled fringe covered part of his blue eyes as he flicked it over with a gentle hand. She knew he had a big heart.

After twenty minutes of small talk and a much-needed distraction, her phone vibrated on the table. It was Gianni. Her heart pounded.

"Answer it, girl."

Rose frowned. "Why is he ringing?" Luna shrugged. "Gianni? Is everything all right?"

"I wanted to see you at the airport and confirm your flight details."

Wouldn't it be that much harder to say goodbye? But then again, she yearned to see him one last time. "Okay." She heard sounds of car horns in the background. "Where are you?"

"I had a last-minute work problem in Florence and am hoping to sort it out tonight. It's been more difficult than I expected, so here's hoping it'll be done and dusted before you leave. I wanted to say goodbye."

Why did he sound cold? "I see." She recited her details. "See you then".

"Bye, and thanks, Rose."

She rubbed her throat after ending the call, feeling parched. "He wants to see me at the airport, but isn't it best he doesn't come? It'll be hard to see him again."

"I know, but it'll give you proper closure." Luna reached for her hand with a reassuring smile. "I am sorry about Gianni. I wish it could work out for you guys."

Rose looked over at Luna, whose eyes remained fixed on hers. "I will miss him. But I'm sure that once I get back I'll be busy, and hopefully forget about him in time." But did a part of her want them to try and have a long-distance relationship? Or was it best to finish it and say their last goodbye? She tried to ignore the empty pit in her stomach.

"You'll be all right, but please keep in touch, girl. I might just come for a surprise visit one day. Miracles have happened."

Rose laughed, knowing she'd miss her friend.

A warmth in her heart gave her hope that she would at least get to see Gianni one more time.

"Listen, Domenico. I appreciate your concerns, but despite the costs, it'll be more financially viable in the long run." Despite talking business, his mind was on Rose and the phone call he had made earlier. He hoped he'd get this issue sorted so he could say goodbye to her at the airport.

He had to see her one last time, even knowing that it would be gut-wrenching to know he could never have her.

Domenico was a broad-shouldered man with huge biceps and piercing, dark eyes. He looked like a bodyguard rather than a businessman, his shirt tight against his heavy chest. "Can you guarantee this projection? I don't see us getting a return for at least five years, possibly more."

Gianni's headache increased as he pushed forward, his elbows on the conference table as he gripped his hands together. At this rate, he wouldn't be finished by the time Rose left. "I've always used property development software and have a set budget in mind. If we keep to those budgets and do close monitoring, I have at least an 80% guarantee that we can have an ROI within two to three years."

"Hmm." He fiddled with his jaw and peered past him. "Show me the software."

He nodded. "Of course. But first, I need to tell you that I have to wrap this up today, as I have an important meeting tomorrow."

Domenico's eyes darkened. "Right. Well, important or not, you need to convince me that I should still contribute my hard-earned money as an investor. Is this meeting business-related?"

Gianni was tempted to lie, but he never acted in an unethical or manipulative manner. He preferred to do honest business. "It's personal."

He nodded. "I would think you'd want to get your priorities in place, given we're talking about a load of money and a long period of construction."

"I understand, but I imagine you'd struggle to work when a woman you deeply care about is always on your mind?"

Domenico's eyes lit up as he smiled to himself, softening. "I might remember, but we still have a lot of work to get through."

At least he wasn't pulling out on the project, but Gianni had to keep him on side. "I can assure you, Domenico, I have the utmost respect for your investment, and plan to make it extremely lucrative for all of us."

"Good to hear. Now let's see this software, and wow me again with your budgeting plan. We should finish soon."

He sighed with relief. "Of course." He reached for his laptop from the smaller table and placed it in front of him, then clicked into the app.

CHAPTER 34

Rose was roused from sleep when the phone on the bedside table buzzed the next morning. It was a text from Gianni. *In case I'm running late today because of work, can you please not board until the very last minute? I need to see you.*

She took a breath when another text came. *The investor needs more convincing about building plans, which means I have to restart my presentation over again. Sorry, but this is important, Rose. It affects contractors, employees, and the Chianti community.*

She texted him back. *Okay. Will wait until the last boarding call. Hope to see you later tonight.*

Rose got up and put on her robe, then headed to the kitchen. Swinging open the fridge, she pulled out two eggs and a pan and poured oil into it. She cracked the eggs and cooked them.

Thoughts of seeing Gianni again brought heat to her chest, but her stomach felt rock hard at the idea she'd no longer see him after this afternoon. She fought against a weakness in her legs as she sat down and attempted to eat her eggs.

Despite Luna offering to get one of her friends involved in managing the retreat, it wasn't workable, given her tenuous relationship with the man she had fallen hopelessly in love with.

Rose ate her eggs mindfully, an image of Gianni playing over in her mind. Shaking out her thoughts, she stood in front of the sink, feeling as if she had heavy weights pulling her down. Tears ran down her face as she realised that she would never see the man of her dreams again once she arrived in Melbourne. Never feel the brush of his tongue against her neck. Never feel the caress of his hands against her cheeks. Never again have his hands brush through her hair as if he couldn't get enough of her. How would she live without him?

Wiping away her tears, she soaped a sponge and rubbed it over her plate, remembering his kindness and the way he had showered her with gifts, as if she deserved such extravagance. How could any of his ex-girlfriends not know the real man behind his billionaire status? How could he believe she wouldn't care about him if he wasn't wealthy?

She put him out of her mind, headed to the bathroom and mindlessly brushed her teeth before showering to get ready for her last morning with the writing students, who were bringing refreshments to say goodbye.

Half an hour later, she stood opposite her desk and addressed her students. "I'd like you to tell me how you plan to publish your piece of work. I know some of you have written proposals to publishers, but others plan to self-publish. It's important to know the difference." A show of hands around the room led to replies about most students wishing to self-publish. "As most of you want to be independent, I'm handing out a document outlining the steps involved with distribution, editing, formatting, and design. There's even an estimated cost, and links to services."

Julie grinned. "This is great, Rose. Extremely helpful." She looked around the room. "We're all going to miss you. But what about your writers' retreat? Are you still planning to open that up one day? I think all of us would be interested." Nodding heads lifted her spirits.

Her stomach quailed at the thought that she'd given them hope and was now dashing it. "I've cut it loose. It's not practical. I'd struggle finding someone to run it when I don't live here."

Julie leaned forward. "You could stay here and run it yourself."

Rose sat back at her desk and rummaged through a pile of papers, her eyes downcast. Her life couldn't change so drastically. Italy would soon be her past. "My life's in Melbourne, Julie."

"I know of a few literary friends who might want to run it," Julie said.

"I appreciate that. If anything changes, I'll let you guys know. I have all your contact details and will keep in touch.'"

Why did she feel like she'd be letting the writing community down? It'd be a dream come true, but a logistical nightmare.

The students headed to a table filled with assorted hot foods, pizzas, confectionary, sweet breads and bottles of wine as Rose joined them.

No, her life was in Australia.

CHAPTER 35

G ianni ran from one end of the airport to the boarding gate, hoping that Rose hadn't yet left. She'd promised she'd be the last one to board.

He pushed through crowds ambling along the glossy floors and bumped into a man who refused to move. "I'm in a rush. Please move."

The man shot him a dirty look. "Well, aren't we all in a blood hurry?" He shook his head in disgust.

Looking up at the timetable, he ignored people shoving past him and winced. The plane hadn't left yet, but could he possibly get to her before she boarded?

Two people stood in line, but Rose was nowhere to be found. Had she already boarded the plane? His heart felt like it was shrinking, and a sudden onset of nausea made him bow his head. Had he missed his chance?

If he didn't get to see her one last time, it would break his heart. He had a lot to tell her and had reconsidered their relationship. His heart shifted as if it would explode right out of his chest, his panic heightening.

Gianni was about to approach the stern-looking woman behind the counter when he spotted Rose behind a post as she slowly made her way towards him. She spoke to the ground hostess. "I'll only be a few minutes, then I'll board."

The lady nodded. "Okay, but hurry or the plane will take off without you."

Rose approached him. "Thanks for coming."

"I am so sorry." He edged closer and yearned to kiss her but held back. Her shoulders drooped and her eyes became misty. "The investor took longer than expected, but listen, Rose, I was thinking." He took a breath. "Maybe we could make it work. The investor said he had started out having a distant, long-term relationship himself. But later, they compromised and spent six months of the year together until they married."

She shook her head. "That's ridiculous, Gianni. I can't afford to come here every six months. Not all of us are billionaires."

"But don't you see? I could fund it. Maybe if I came to Australia for six months and worked remotely until I returned to Italy. I could pay for you to come here in the alternate six months."

"Gianni, this is madness. I'm about to leave and you spring this on me now? Weren't you the one who said we were a fantasy and agreed to end it?"

Gianni leaned forward. "I didn't mean any of that. I was hurting, and I had to push aside my love for you to survive. I love you, Rose."

Rose shuffled her feet and shoved her hands in her pants pockets. Her eyes misted and her bottom lip trembled as she gazed deeply into his eyes, as if she was about to break. His heart went out to her, and he just wanted to hold her.

But then, with a deep sigh she hardened, as if pushing all emotions aside. "I can't talk about this right now. I have to go. Like I said, this could never work... As much as... As I..."

He cocked his head. "As much as you what, Rose?" Was she about to tell him she loved him too? Did she share his feelings?

"Nothing, but without sounding like a broken record, we have to end it now."

Gianni clutched his arms to his chest, fighting the ache. "No, I don't believe that, Rose. I love you, dammit. Tell me you don't love me and I'll walk away right now. Tell me."

Rose averted her eyes, then faced him with a lone tear running down her cheek. "I love you too, Gianni, but it's not enough. It can never be enough, and I'm sorry."

The woman at the counter behind her said, "Miss, you need to board now."

Rose nodded. "I have to go." They pulled into a tight embrace and shed tears. "I'm sorry."

Gianni nodded as he avoided her eyes. "I'm sorry too. For everything."

Rose raced over to the boarding gates without looking back. She was gone.

Gianni stared into space for what seemed like hours, gripping his elbows at his sides. He vowed to never get involved with a woman ever again. He was done. He couldn't even describe the depth of the stabbing pain in his chest.

Rose walked through the gates with a hunched posture as she pushed aside her grief and stepped on board the plane. She gripped the strap of her bag while carrying her backpack in her other hand.

She sighed heavily with her stomach clenching and breath hitching. She had thought she'd miss her chance to see Gianni and had felt sick. Would it be the universe telling them they weren't meant to be together?

Her rejection of Gianni hurt like hell but loving him and then possibly losing him would be more gut-wrenching. She was sick of losing people she loved: her father, her great aunt, ex-boyfriends. She couldn't take such a chance with Gianni.

She stood behind a passenger who took his time, shoving his baggage into the overhead compartment while the noise in the cabin sharpened the pounding in her head. Why did she feel like someone had died? In truth, her relationship with Gianni had died, and she'd need a long time to recover.

Rose pushed her backpack into the compartment, then sat in her window seat, nervously anticipating the final take-off of her plane. She missed her family and friends in Melbourne, but knew she'd be leaving someone important back in Italy. If she stopped thinking about him, she'd be fine. She would not break down on the plane.

Once most of the passengers were in their seats, she scrolled through her phone and read his last text message, as if those words would keep him alive in her heart. *I will always love you, Rose. I'll never forget you.*

Attempting to numb her feelings, she waited for the people to get settled into their seats and picked up her book. Distractions would help take her mind off her aching heart.

CHAPTER 36

Gianni knocked on the door as he shifted his posture, shuffling his feet. He stared at the quaint cottage-style home.

He had taken in the vast wide roads in the busy city from the Tullamarine Airport, huge compared to the narrow streets and small roads in Italy. The chilly wind gave him little comfort.

Despite having travelled to many countries for work, he had never been to Melbourne.

When the door opened, Rose flinched, and her eyes dilated. "Gianni? What...What are you doing here?"

He reached for her hands, and she accepted them hesitantly. "I couldn't stay away."

She winced. "But we said our goodbyes." Her eyes gazed at him from head to toe as if they told her something different.

Gianni laughed. "Can I come in, or do you plan to stare at me standing here all day?"

She blushed. "Of course." She pulled the door open wider. "This is a surprise."

He walked inside as he gazed at the open, spacious kitchen with glossy cupboards and an island counter with stools behind it. A glossy timber table was centred in an open dining area with padded steel chairs. French doors opened to reveal a large backyard, a trampoline, and potted plants. Her laptop and piles of notebooks, manila folders, and stationery were placed on the table. "You have a beautiful home."

Rose pushed her belongings to one side. "Thanks. Take a seat. I'll get you a drink. What would you like?"

"Water's fine." He sat at the table and waited with bated breath, noticing her hand shaking as she pushed the glass of iced water towards him.

She sat opposite him. "How was your flight?"

"Too long. I didn't realise how far away you lived." His chest was about to explode with nerves and his head throbbed. *Just tell her.*

"I know. It's as if you'll never arrive, and when you do, it's magic."

"It sure is," he said.

Rose tapped her fingers and averted her eyes.

Gianni's heart felt heavy, and his throat dry despite sipping his water that failed to refresh it. The darkness in her eyes made him want to wrap his arms around her, telling her it would all work out. But could it? Did she still not trust him?

Rose lifted her eyes, and they locked with his. She squeezed her hands together before resting them on her lap, a redness growing around her throat. Was she as nervous as he was? "I can't believe it's been a month already." She got up. "I need a drink."

She filled a glass of water from the tap and spilled some on the ground. He watched her wiping it with a paper towel before turning back around, not wanting her to see him gaze in her direction. "We need to talk, Rose. About us." Rose took her seat beside him, peering past him. "I... I missed you."

A tear fell down her cheek. "What?"

He reached for her hands, and she squeezed his. "I realised you weren't like the others when you turned down the money for the villa. You didn't care about wealth but about saving your family's legacy. The memories you shared and the love you experienced—I admire that." His heart raced. "I will say this again, Rose." He swallowed. "I'm not a greedy developer or billionaire who's cold and ruthless. Not that I blame you for thinking we were all alike after what your aunt went through." He exhaled. "I truly am sorry for lying to you, Rose. I needed you to see me for me, and to have a voice as Gianni the man, and not as anything else."

Rose took a deep breath. "I would never have seen you as greedy when we first met, Gianni."

He shook his head. "I didn't know that at the time. I was scared to commit, I admit, but also because my father never gave me a voice and only cared whenever I pleased him. Now, I realise that he loves me in his own way. You've changed me for the better, Rose."

Rose stared into her hands. "I have?"

He nodded. "I love you, Rose, and cannot live without you. You keep me awake at night. Each morning, you're on my mind. I want to share my life with you. I want to wake up beside you and sleep with you every night. I want us to watch crazy TV together, make love in front of a fireplace, shower together, cook together, and talk until the middle of the night. I want to grow old with you after we have gorgeous babies who look like you and are as smart and savvy as you."

Tears flowed down her cheeks. "Oh, Gianni. I love you too. So much it hurts. But we live twenty fours away from each other."

"I know I sprung the decision about commuting at the airport, but why don't we trial it? If it doesn't work, it doesn't work."

Her eyes darkened. "If it doesn't work, Gianni, I don't know if I can bear it. It's been hard living without you, but what if things go wrong and there's more heartbreak?"

"I know there are no guarantees, but I believe wholeheartedly that you and I love each other enough to make sacrifices. Can you take a chance on us? On our love?"

Rose's eyes darted past him, pondering. "Does that mean you're here to stay for six months, or do you want me to get back to Italy later? I won't be relying on your money, Gianni. I could try to come back in a year."

"Let's take it one month at a time, and review in six months. I'm here to stay if you'll have me. I don't mind finding an apartment nearby."

Rose beamed. "No need. There's plenty of room in my bed, Gianni."

He leaned forward and smashed his lips against hers. Rose pulled away and guided him towards the bedroom, knowing she was about to love him like he had never been loved in a new country.

EPILOGUE

SIX MONTHS LATER

R ose shifted in her stance as she greeted her last
guest for the morning. "Welcome to the writer's
retreat at Terrini's Guesthouse. Daniella will take you
to your room to get settled and give you the day's
schedule. There is a writer's class in two hours, just
before lunch."

She had established the guesthouse with the help of
Gianni's property development skills, and he'd invested
in her business as a partner. Rose was now living in
Montepulciano but planned to visit her family and
friends in Melbourne when time or money allowed.

The guests talked amongst themselves and stood near
Daniella, who was a friend of Luna's, working with
Rose on a part-time basis at the retreat. She threaded a
hand through her blonde curls as she winked in Rose's
direction while walking off with the guests.

Gianni stood beside her. "I can't believe you just got your first ten guests. Wow! It's already looking lucrative from my end."

Rose stood in the living room and plonked herself on the sofa. "Thanks to your development expertise. The villa's got that extra room, which you got done so quickly, and I can't believe I've got one staff member already. How can I ever thank you?"

Gianni beamed. "I should thank you for intervening with my father. Our relationship's still a work in progress, but you've made him realise the error of his ways."

She waved a hand. "Oh, it's nothing. Even your father has a soft side. But the more I get to know you, the more I fall in love with you."

"Same here, gorgeous. I cannot believe you're living here now. You must miss your friends, your mum."

She nodded. "I do, but if this business does well, I can see them more often. I realised I had always missed my first home, and Montepulciano was my first home."

"This is amazing." His eyes turned to the staircase as Daniella came down.

"I'll be in the kitchen, confirming the day trips for tomorrow," Daniella said. She frowned at Gianni. What was going on?

"No worries, Daniella. Thanks for that," said Rose.

"Let's go outside," said Gianni. He led her towards a wilting tree and breathed heavily. He pulled out a box and opened it with a click.

She gasped, staring wide-eyed at a ruby red diamond nestled in a gold ring. "What the hell?"

He went down on one knee and held the ring aloft while her legs wobbled beneath her. "Rose, I have loved you more and more every day. I've seen your inner and outer beauty, the way you love and care for others, the way you're quick to learn, especially with your new business, your success as an author, and the way you love, and teach me new things every day. Rose, I love you so much I cannot breathe. It's like I can never get enough of you, never get close enough to you. You're a part of me and I'm a part of you, hopefully. I love you, darling, and want you to marry me. Be my wife and let's grow old together."

Rose cried. "Oh, Gianni. Of course I'll marry you. You are my light."

Gianni stood and planted his lips on hers as he hungrily delved into her mouth. "You're my light too." In a tight embrace, they held each other until they made their way back inside with their arms around one another.

The sun shone, and the spring in their steps gave them the surety that despite life's challenges, they'd get through them together in love.

Reviews are GOLD to authors. If you enjoyed this book, please consider leaving a review at:

https://mybook.to/TwoHeartsVilla

Check out Dalia's Story in *Risk To The Heart*, Book 1 of the Billionaire Romance Series below:

https://mybook.to/Risk-to-the-Heart

ABOUT THE AUTHOR

Lucy Appadoo is the author of contemporary romance novels and the billionaire romance series alongside the Friends In Crisis and Women Of Strength series in the romantic suspense genre.

After a childhood spent reading and imagining escapist worlds, Lucy has put her imagination into stories. Her work as a rehabilitation counsellor, and former work as a counsellor in private practice, have led to an interest in writing inspirational stories about authentic, driven women who manage adversity with strength and heart.

Lucy's interests include plotting the next love story, researching crime stories and news to inspire her work, watching crime thrillers and suspenseful movies, travel, exercising, reading for entertainment or knowledge, meditation, and spending time with friends and family.

She also appreciates her Italian background and culture, which has inspired her to write imaginative stories about her parents' childhoods that have led to The Italian Family Series novels.

Check out Lucy's website and sign up for a free exclusive suspenseful novella below:

https://www.lucyappadooauthor.com.au

ALSO BY LUCY APPADOO

FICTION

Billionaire Romance Series

Risk To The Heart (Book 1):

https://mybook.to/Risk-to-the-Heart

Contemporary Romance – Stand-alone

Second Chances: http://mybook.to/Secondchance

A Tuscan Dream: https://mybook.to/ATuscanDream

Women Of Strength Series – Romantic Suspense/Thriller

In Rio's Shadows (Book 1):

https://books2read.com/u/mq1qP8

Shadows Of The Past (Book 2):

https://books2read.com/u/3JZe1X

Secrets In The Shadows (Book 3):
https://books2read.com/u/ml88kv

Friends In Crisis Series - Romantic Suspense/Thriller

Haunted By The Past (Book 1):
https://books2read.com/u/bw2ZeY
Twisted Obsession (Book 2):
https://books2read.com/u/4DW8pk
Web Of Lies (Book 3):
https://books2read.com/u/3JXazE
Love-Obsessed (Book 4):
https://books2read.com/u/4jPKGX
Fatal Designs (Book 5):
https://books2read.com/u/3nBjy5

The Hearts Series - Romantic Suspense

Rising Hearts (Book 1):
https://books2read.com/u/mZwpoE
Forbidden Hearts (Book 2):
https://books2read.com/u/bQBKr7
Kindred Hearts (Book 3):
https://books2read.com/u/4AJKQK
Broken Hearts (prequel to Forbidden Hearts):
https://books2read.com/u/mgrnOD

Short Story Thrillers

Evening Interrupted:

https://books2read.com/u/3yZDjZ

The Dreamcatcher: https://books2read.com/u/bzaLxn

Red Flags: https://books2read.com/u/bWZ9W1

Collection of Short Story Thrillers:

https://books2read.com/u/bP5vwj

The Italian Family Series - Coming of Age Family Drama/Romance

A New Life: https://books2read.com/u/mqqwZm

The Beauty of Tears: https://books2read.com/u/bpqwk3

Dancing in the Rain:

https://books2read.com/u/bOr7LA

A Life By Design: https://books2read.com/u/3J8ene

NON-FICTION

Grief & Loss

Moving Beyond Grief - How To Shift From Grief & Loss to Joy & Peace: https://books2read.com/u/mVNzDA

Stress Management & Anxiety

Holistic Spiritual and Mental Health - Building Resilience and Creativity by Conquering Anxiety and Managing Stress: https://books2read.com/u/47kG8A

Career Guidance

Your Holistic Career Path - Create Career
Change, Satisfaction, and Work/Life Balance:
https://books2read.com/u/bzYDz4